Funny Business

THE MUSICAL

Book by Rachel Brittain
& Daniel Falk

Music and Lyrics by
Daniel Abrahamson

A SAMUEL FRENCH ACTING EDITION

SAMUEL
FRENCH
FOUNDED 1830
NEW YORK HOLLYWOOD LONDON TORONTO

SAMUELFRENCH.COM

ISBN 978-0-573-69613-8   Printed in U.S.A.   #8240

IMPORTANT BILLING AND CREDIT REQUIREMENTS

All producers of *FUNNY BUSINESS must* give credit to the Author of the Play in all programs distributed in connection with performances of the Play, and in all instances in which the title of the Play appears for the purposes of advertising, publicizing or otherwise exploiting the Play and/or a production. The name of the Author *must* appear on a separate line on which no other name appears, immediately following the title and *must* appear in size of type not less than fifty percent of the size of the title type.

FUNNY BUSINESS - THE MUSICAL was produced at the Diesel Playhouse in Toronto, Canada, in 2007. The production was directed by Marc Richard, with musical direction by Konrad Pluta, set and costumes by Dennis Horn, and lighting design by Sandra Marcroft. The cast was as follows:

STUART	J. Sean Elliott
DIANE	Alison Woolridge
MARCUS	Chris Trussell
JACK	Trevor Campbell
BRIE	Lana Carillo

CHARACTERS

STUART (40s) – A befuddled yet loveable boss.
JACK (20s) – A nerdy but guitar-playing intern.
BRIE (20s) – A chatty and pretty receptionist.
DIANE (late 30s) – A hot and tough as nails marketing manager.
MARCUS (late 30s) – A slick salesman.

TIME, PLACE, AND SETTING

The night of the Chime Canada Team Building Talent Show.
Toronto, Canada, 2008.

AUTHORS' NOTE

Let me set the stage for you: it was November 2006 in Toronto, which meant our beautiful city was heading into our eight-month winter and three young music theatre graduates were doing what most music theatre graduates were doing in November in Toronto: temping.

Twice a week, the team would gather at Starbucks with laptops in tow and share our stories of office drama. We'd frequently finish our rant with this exasperated exclamation, "Honestly, guys, you can't WRITE this sh*t!"

That is where the journey of *Funny Business – The Musical* began; within the dimly lit corridors and catty little cubicles of corporate Canada where myself and my writing partners would while away our days filing papers, getting coffee and secretly taking notes.

Once we had made the decision that, "Doggone it, we're going to write a musical!", it was full speed ahead. As new writers, we held ourselves to tight deadlines and fast turnaround. From January to May, we were writing a new draft every 14 days. We gathered our friends to do readings every month, with the promise of beer and pizza. But the most crucial development tool in our process wasn't born in our Theatre History class. We borrowed from the business world.

Focus groups were held during pivotal points of the script development. We invited people from many of the major downtown corporations to attend and asked them to provide feedback via forms we distributed to each and every person. The information we gathered from these focus groups provided invaluable insight into our work and how we were going to relate to our audiences. We didn't want to write a show that simply made fun of a corporate world that we didn't understand – an artist's take on a world they didn't belong to – but instead to write the show from the inside out that lovingly lampooned the nine-to-five life.

Funny Business – The Musical first opened at the 2007 Toronto Fringe to – thankfully – rave reviews and much buzz. With as much gusto as we could muster for being all under the age of 25, we grabbed up our Fringe cast and took the show straight downtown (Diesel Playhouse) to open a full-scale professional production in Toronto.

I could now proceed to explain to you how much grey hair we earned during those five months at the Diesel Playhouse; how we battled timing, weather, ticket prices, recessions, theatre owners, critics and parents to make *Funny Business* fly for as long as it could; but instead, I'll let you imagine what it may have been like for us young people fighting the good fight for commercial theatre in Toronto. I say that with much affection.

Bottom line, it was 125 performances after opening that the curtain finally fell on *Funny Business – The Musical*. It was and continues to be one of the most life-altering experiences that any of us has gone through and we couldn't be more grateful. But enough about us – let's get back to business.

- Rachel Brittain
2009

MUSICAL NUMBERS

Act I

1. Overtime Overture .... Felix
2. Funny Business .... Ensemble
3. High Speed Lan .... Jack
4. Just Like Jack .... Brie
4. Live a Little Better .... Marcus, Diane
5. Keep it Together .... Ensemble
6. The Stratango .... Marcus and Diane
7. The Sales Guy .... Marcus
8. Welcome to the Business .... Marcus, Diane, Jack, Brie
9. Keep it Together Reprise .... Stuart
10. Now it's Personal .... Diane
11. Out to Dry .... Ensemble

Act II

12. It's My First Day .... Marcus, Diane, Jack, Brie
13. Tour the World in Toronto .... Marcus, Diane
14. Bottom Line .... Jack, Brie
15. You Can't Fire Me (I Quit!) .... Ensemble
16. Back to Business .... Ensemble

ACT I – DRESS REHEARSAL

SCENE ONE – Meet the Team

(FELIX enters. Starts to play the overture.)

STUART. *(voice over, interrupting)* Is this on? Oh. Hi Felix. No, don't stop playing. Every show needs an overture and you really need the practice. Don't worry, I won't interrupt you during the actual show. That would be weird. Gosh, it's dark back here. What does this do?

(The house lights turn on and off.)

Nope. That's not it. Just wanted to tell you that we got the sprinklers turned off back stage. Don't worry – nobody is on fire anymore. I guess the smoke machine is officially a no go. Woo, that's spooky music, Felix. Anyway, there is still time for the dress rehearsal before the audience gets here. I'm going to be out there any minute to do my opening remarks. Wait. Clean up on aisle three. Ha, ha. I've always wanted to say that. Okay, bye!

(STUART enters. FELIX plays some wrong notes.)

That ending needs a little work.

FELIX. Please tell me this counts as overtime.

STUART. This could be your ticket out of the mail room. Alright, let's get started. Ah, yes, cue cards. Cue cards. Welcome Toronto Branch of Chime Communications Canada to our team-building talent show which I have affectionately coined 'Funny Business!' What a turn-out! I guess you got the memo. Ha, ha. Anyway, head office is going to be so pleased. First off, thank you all for your mandatory submissions into the Talent Hat – your coworkers performing for you tonight have been chosen at random. All we ask of you is that you relax, have a drink or two, and encourage your fellow office friends with your applause.

(**BRIE** *enters.*)

BRIE. Do we come out now?

STUART. No, not yet! I still have to say, 'How are you all feeling tonight?' and they'll say, 'Good!' And then I'll ask them if they're ready to get down, and they'll go 'Yeah!' and then when they'll all riled up, I throw my hands up in the air like this and scream, 'Are you ready for some team-building?"

DIANE. Stuart, this dress rehearsal is cutting into my smoke break. Step it up.

STUART. Okay, okay! Without any further adieu, I present your team members here at Chime! And now Brie, you come out now and introduce yourself.

BRIE. Okay. Hi! You all know me. I'm Brie, the Receptionist. I type 97 words per minute and I have over 600 friends on Facebook.

STUART. Oh, and I'll mention that because you're away from your desk, I've forwarded all reception calls to your personal cell phone.

BRIE. You did what?!

STUART. Jack!

(**JACK** *enters.*)

JACK. Hi, I'm Jack the intern. I'm currently implementing a cluster analysis system through a Bartlet Window to actuate the minimum aberration of bimodal, and/or Asymmetrical distribution…

STUART. That was thorough! But…

BRIE. You should say something funny or cute about yourself.

JACK. But I'm not funny or cute. I work in finance.

STUART. Jack, why don't you tell the audience about the puppet show you're doing with Brie or that surprise guitar song for Br – ?

JACK. Uh, yeah. The puppet show. That's a good idea. Hi. I'm Jack. Brie and I will be puppet-ing tonight. Puppet-ing. Is that even a word?

STUART. Come on, Jack, we've only got – time check!

(The LCD flashes "50:10" on the screen.)

– fifty minutes and five seconds til they open those doors! By the way, Kevin from IT will be up in the booth helping us out all night. Say 'Hi!', Kevin.

KEVIN. *(typing via LCD screen)* HI.

STUART. That's so cool. Thanks for helping out tonight, Kevin…especially since this is your last day with us and you should be at home packing your bags. I'll let everyone know that Noelle from Quality Assurance is bringing a cake for after. Where did I transfer you to again?

KEVIN. *(typing)* WINNIPEG.

STUART. You'd better bring a sweater! Ha, ha. Oh, I'm kidding. You'll love it there.

KEVIN. *(typing)* …

STUART. Who's next?

DIANE. I'm Diane. I run the marketing department. I was lucky enough to get picked yadda yadda yadda, now I'm stuck doing a ridiculous salsa duet. Enjoy your damn cocktails.

STUART. Sounds like someone's got a case of the pricklies! Now, Diane, you wouldn't say that in front of your co-workers!

DIANE. I wouldn't do a salsa either.

STUART. It's gonna be fun!

DIANE. The weekend in Banff would have been fun. This is torture.

STUART. Don't be such a debbie downer. Marcus! You're up!

MARCUS. Hey, I'm Marcus, in Sales. Office MVP 2001 – 2004. Emma – you're looking beautiful as always. Josh, love the new tie. Larry – is that your lovely wife or your daughter? Ha ha – sure she is.

STUART. Very good, Marcus. Jack, you see? That was – (very endearing).

DIANE. – What the hell are you doing?

MARCUS. I'm practicing! Gotta woo my audience.

DIANE. You can't woo.

MARCUS. I woo better than you. And I rhymed. Man, I'm good.

STUART. Come on, you two. You're both pretty.

(He looks at DIANE, indicating her face.)

Ooh. Shiny.

And now I'd like to tell you about how this magical evening came to pass. On the recent management retreat in Puerto Plata, the CEO was going over the results of my 360 degree review, and he wisely said to me, "Stuart, fix your branch!" And I said, "Sir, that's food for thought." So I sat on the beach for a few days to gain some clarity – the kind of clarity you can only get from an all-inclusive resort – and then it hit me. I put down my mai tai and said, "What we need is a good old-fashioned shot in the arm of Vitamin 'team-building'!" But how? Just then, an adorable clump of local children were in front of me, dancing for spare change. Sadly ironic because, as I said, it was an all-inclusive and nobody was carrying any money on them. Either way, I got inspired. I thought, who needs a weekend in Banff? Toronto is all about the three T's: the TSX, the TTC, and the T-H-E-A-T-E-R –

BRIE. R–E

STUART. R-E. So why not put on a talent show? Now, there's been a few questions like, "Why?" and, "How does this help morale?", and "Should you be calling me at home?" Well, tonight is about having fun! I mean, sure…uh, Felix, that's your cue to start the music for the opening number…that's okay, we're all on a learning curve here. I'll feed you line again. Tonight is about having fun! I mean, sure…

SCENE TWO – Funny Business Opening

SONG – "FUNNY BUSINESS"

STUART.

> THERE'S NOT MUCH TO LAUGH AT IN THE WORLD
> TODAY
> WITH ALL THAT'S GOING ON
> THE ECONOMY'S LAGGING, YOU'VE GOT BILLS TO
> PAY
> YOUR SEX LIFE MAKES YOU YAWN
>
> OUR MORALE IS DEPLETING
> SO I'VE CALLED THIS MEETING
> TO ACT BEFORE IT'S GONE
> THERE'S LOTS OF FUNNY BUSINESS GOING ON
>
> Hit it!

JACK.

> THERE'S TERROR AND TROUBLE IN THE MIDDLE
> EAST

BRIE.

> AND A NEVER ENDING WAR

MARCUS.

> THE GLOBE IS WARMING

DIANE.

> AND WE'RE RUNNING LOW ON OIL

STUART.

> BUT THAT'S EASY TO IGNORE

ALL.

> THERE'S TOO MUCH DEPRESSION
> IN OUR CHOSEN PROFESSION
> SO TONIGHT LET'S HAVE SOME FUN!
> THERE'S LOTS OF FUNNY BUSINESS GOING ON

STUART. Pulled randomly from the Talent Hat, your fellow coworkers here at Chime! Starting with…

ALL. Brie!

JACK. The Receptionist – knows everybody's name

STUART. You could eat her with an apple!

JACK. Stuart –

STUART. What?

BRIE. That's kinda lame.

ALL. Marcus!

BRIE. In Sales he's pretty cool and slick –

MARCUS. I could sell snow to an eskimo!

DIANE. He's also kind of thick.

ALL. Diane!

MARCUS. Head of Marketing. She's making all the calls.

BRIE. She'll delegate, litigate

JACK. And really bust your balls.

ALL. Jack – the Intern!

(All hum and ha over what JACK does.)

JACK. Guys, I've been here almost a year. You really should know –

ALL. Stuart – the boss!

STUART. That's me! The leader of this team. I'm respected, loved and capable!

ALL. *(except STUART)* In his wildest dreams!

STUART. Welcome to the Sage Theatre! Now on with the show!

ALL.

YOU MIGHT NOT BE LAUGHING AS YOU'RE HEADED TO WORK

YOU MIGHT DREAD EACH DAWN

THE BOREDOM IS RAMPANT AND YOU'RE GOING BERSERK

BUT THIS YOU CAN COUNT ON

WHETHER DOWN IN THE MAIL ROOM

OR UP IN THE BOARDROOM

OR THE PLANT THAT'S IN TAIWAN

THERE'S LOTS OF FUNNY BUSINESS GOING ON!

THERE'S LOTS OF FUNNY BUSINESS

STUART. Big finish!

GOING ON!

SCENE THREE – Sales versus Marketing

STUART. *(cont.)* Wonderful! Wait for applause. And then I'll say: up next will be a salsa by the very exotic and erotic Diane and Marcus.

(LCD: HOSTILE WORKPLACE LANGUAGE!)

What's that?

JACK. I think it's an alarm. Looks like Jerry from Human Resources is up in the tech booth with Kevin.

BRIE. Your use of the word erotic has probably been deemed inappropriate.

STUART. Oh. Jerry from HR. Right, gotcha. Well, then, forget erotic. It's very sensual…

(LCD: HOSTILE WORKPLACE LANGUAGE!)

– suggestive (!)…civilized?

DIANE. I'm sorry, Stuart, but I'm cancelling the duet.

BRIE. Here they go again.

STUART. Cancelling the duet? What are you talking about?

MARCUS. She's upset over my brilliant costume choices. I'm giving the people what they want. And I know it's about multiculturalism – the global village, very hot right now.

DIANE. A riveting market analysis…from 2006. You'd know that if you read Canadian Business instead of Maxim.

STUART. Ha ha, woooaaah there cowgirl –

(LCD: HOSTILE WORKPLACE LANGUAGE!)

… cow woman? I'm sure this whole thing is just getting blown out of proportion – lemme see your costumes! Jack, why don't you work on your opening remarks?

(MARCUS, DIANE, STUART *and* **BRIE** *exit.)*

SCENE FOUR – Meet a Guy Named Jack

JACK. Hi! Hi. Hi. I'm Jack. Hey I'm Jack Staple. Oh God, I don't know…Jack Staple here, I'm an Intern. I do a lot of things here at Chime, like…

KEVIN. BORING.

JACK. I know…it sounds like a bad profile on Lavalife.

(BRIE enters, carrying a guitar.)

BRIE. Look what I've got!

JACK. My guitar…?!

BRIE. Play something for me!

JACK. Um, well, I wasn't really ready to show you –

BRIE. Come on, Jack! You always promise to play something for me and you never do.

JACK. Okay. Well, I was saving it for tonight…It's still a rough draft. Kevin helped me out with the lyrics. So… let me know what you think. It's about…a girl. Or something.

SONG – "HIGH SPEED LAN"

YOU'RE MY DUAL CORE, 2 GIG PENTIUM C
YOU'RE MY SDRAM, MY 80 GIG HDD
AND IF YOU WANT ME TO BE YOUR MAN
LET'S FIND A COMPATIBLE ROUTER
AND JOIN THE SAME HIGH SPEED LAN
Well?

BRIE. I like it! I do! It's very sweet. Very…technical. You know, you don't need Kevin to help you. I'd write your own lyrics.

JACK. But Kevin thinks –

BRIE. Jack, does Kevin even have a girlfriend?

JACK. No…

BRIE. …and he still lives with his mom.

KEVIN. F…U

BRIE. Wow. Mature. Anyway, all you need to do is speak from your heart.

SCENE FIVE – Stuart Can't Find His Notebook

(STUART enters.)

STUART. Jack, my boy! I need you to boot up that computerized coconut of yours. In all the ker-fluffle about the salsa costumes, I forgot that my stand up act is coming up, and I still can't find my joke book with all my material in it, which I lost during the panic with the sprinkler system. I was running for cover and I got soaked – but not as bad as Brie! You see, Brie, that's why you don't wear white after labour day. See-through! But I swear I didn't look. Come on, Jack we're on a mission! Brie, why don't you help brainstorm something for Jack's opening remarks?

(JACK and STUART exit.)

SCENE SIX – Just Like Jack

SONG – "JUST LIKE JACK"

BRIE.

JACK IS SUCH GOOD GUY WHAT TO TELL YOU
ABOUT JACK.
HE'S FRIENDLY BUT HE'S SHY AND HE ALWAYS HAS
YOUR BACK
HE'S A REAL GOOD LISTENER THOUGH HE DOESN'T
LIKE TO TALK
AND WHEN HE DOES HE USES REALLY BIG WORDS

HE'S MY B F F, THOUGH WE ONLY MET LAST YEAR
AND HE'S ALWAYS UNDERSTANDING AND SWEET
WHEN HE TELLS ME THAT I NEED TO FIND A
CERTAIN KIND OF GUY
WELL, HERE'S THE KIND OF GUY I NEED

HE'D BRING ME MY LUNCH, WHILE I'M AT MY DESK
EACH TIME HE SAW ME CRY
AND SOMEHOW HE'D KNOW I LOVE PEPSI AND
PRINGLES
AND A BIG STEAMING BOWL OF PAD THAI

AND WHEN I'M FEELING DEPRESSED
CAUSE MY HAIR IS A MESS
HE'D QUIETLY RUB MY BACK
SOMEONE WHO'S SMART, WITH PLENTY OF HEART
I NEED SOMEONE JUST LIKE…

I NEED THE KINDA GUY YOU COULD TAKE HOME TO
MOM
EVEN IF HE ISN'T PHILIPINO
MOM WOULD JUST LOVE HIM AND DAD WOULD JUST
STARE
BUT WHO CARES, WHAT DOES HE KNOW!

HE'D BE AWKWARD BUT FUNNY, WOULDN'T CARE
ABOUT MONEY
AND KNOW WHEN TO GET OFF MY BACK
BUT THAT WON'T BE OFTEN CAUSE I ALWAYS SOFTEN

SO I NEED SOMEONE JUST LIKE

BRIE. Jack…Jack!

JACK ALWAYS MAKES ME HAPPY
WHEN THE WORLD IS GETTING ME DOWN
HE COULD KEEP YOUR HEAD IN THE CLOUDS
AND YOUR FEET ON THE GROUND…

OH I CAN'T BELIEVE I COULDN'T SEE
WHAT WAS RIGHT BEFORE MY EYES
I'VE BEEN COMPLETELY BLIND
AND TOTALLY OUT OF MIND
WHEN I WAS WASTING TIME WITH AARON OR ZACH
WHEN ALL I NEED IS A GUY LIKE JACK?

SO THEN IT'S ALL SETTLED, I KNOW WHAT I NEED
AND NOW I'M FINALLY ON TRACK
AND I KNOW EXACTLY HOW TO PROCEED
FIND SOMEONE JUST LIKE JACK.

(**JACK** *enters.*)

JACK. Brie! Stuart is panicking about his missing joke book.
I need your help.

SCENE SEVEN – Anything You Can Do

(**DIANE** *enters, wearing a melon breast plate.*)

DIANE. Brie, you're the receptionist, right –

BRIE. – Yah –

DIANE. – Great. I need you to sew something.

BRIE. Sorry, Jack needs me.

(**BRIE** *and* **JACK** *exit.*)

DIANE. Unbelievable! Ugh – these stupid costumes.

(**MARCUS** *enters.*)

MARCUS. You must be PMS-ing real bad.

DIANE. I sent you a detailed breakdown about this dance, Marcus. These costumes are all wrong!

MARCUS. Well, you didn't need to rip the kiwis off.

DIANE. The bananas's next.

MARCUS. Diane, come on! I did my job! You just wanna chap my hide.

DIANE. I have better uses for my time. Which is more than I can say for those teenage admin assistants you chase.

MARCUS. I don't chase. They come to me, like a flock of sexy little sheep.

(imitating the sheep)

Maaarcus! Maaarcus!

(back to **DIANE***)*

Face it, Diane, you want what I got.

DIANE. A burning sensation when I pee?

MARCUS. That's okay, Diane. I'd lash out too if I was passed over for a Christmas bonus…three years in a row.

DIANE. That's not true.

MARCUS. Oh really? One of my teenage admin assistants works in accounting.

DIANE. Well, then she must know about your flaccid commission earnings.

MARCUS. And it hasn't affected me one bit. I still live like a king. You? You live like a hermit.

DIANE. You wanna do this? Fine. Kevin! We'll get Kevin to keep tabs. Start a new spreadsheet!

(music vamps)

SCENE EIGHT – We're In the Red

(The LCD screens start a spreadsheet.)

SONG – "LIVE A LITTLE BETTER"

DIANE.
> I EARN A B SCALE SALARY
> DONATE TO THE TORONTO ARTS GALLERY
> COMPARED TO PEOPLE YOU KNOW, I'M PRETTY
> WELL TO DO
> I SHOP AT THE ST. LAWRENCE MARKET
> MY CONDO OVERLOOKS HIGH PARK IT
> LOOKS LIKE I LIVE JUST A LITTLE BETTER THAN YOU

MARCUS. Yeah, yeah, yeah. Just remember, if you wanted to buy my wardrobe, you'd have to remortgage that condo.

DIANE. Yes, you dress very well. Where do you shop?

MARCUS. Yorkville.

DIANE. Yorkville got a Wal-Mart?

MARCUS. Ha, ha, ha. The clothes are only the beginning.
> I JUST BOUGHT A BRAND NEW CAR
> LYNARD SKYNARD'S OLD GUITAR
> A MOTOROLA RAZR, THIS NEW BLING AND THIS
> TATTOO
> NOTHING I OWN IS MODERATE
> AND MY CONDO'S RIGHT ON THE WATER IT
> LOOKS LIKE I LIVE JUST A LITTLE BETTER THAN YOU

DIANE. I gave a thousand to Sick Kids last year.

MARCUS. I gave two thousand to the Canadian Cancer Society!

DIANE. I gave three thousand to build a well in Africa!

MARCUS. I gave a dollar to every homeless person I passed on Queen Street!

> *(**MARCUS**' total jumps up from fourteen dollars, to one hundred and forty, to fourteen hundred and finally to fourteen thousand in a matter of seconds.)*

DIANE.
I VACATION IN EUROPE

MARCUS.
I DO AN ALL-INCLUSIVE TWICE A YEAR
I HAVE THE SLICKEST JOB

DIANE.
YEAH AND I HAVE A CAREER

BOTH.
NOW DON'T BE GETTING JEALOUS
CAUSE YOU FEEL LOWER CLASS

MARCUS.
I'M THE OFFICE MVP

DIANE.
I'M MORE SENIOR

MARCUS.
YOU GOT THAT RIGHT

DIANE.
YOU'RE AN ASS

My dinnerware is Versace. Five hundred dollars a plate.

MARCUS. I own a boat.

DIANE. A cottage in the Muskokas.

MARCUS. A Playstation 3.

DIANE. I've have a Picasso!!

(**DIANE***'s total leaps up by a hundred and ten million dollars.*)

Well…it's a lithograph.

(*The score drops down to one hundred and ten dollars.*)

MARCUS.
IT'S OBVIOUS I'VE SEEN YOUR BEST

DIANE.
I'VE SEEN YOURS AND I'M NOT IMPRESSED

BOTH.
IT'S CLEAR TO ME WHO'S WON
IT'LL BE PRETTY HARD TO MISCONSTRUE – OO!
THERE'S NOTHING MORE TO SAY
SO CHECK OUT THE DISPLAY

MARCUS.

 IT LOOKS LIKE I LIVE JUST A LITTLE BETTER THAN

DIANE.

 IT'S CLEAR TO ME I LIVE A LITTLE BETTER THAN

BOTH.

 WELL LET'S JUST SEE WHO LIVES A LITTLE BETTER
THAN

 (The LCD displays the totals. **DIANE** *and* **MARCUS** *are in the red.)*

 WHAT?!

DIANE. That – that can't be right…What about my savings?

KEVIN. EMPTY.

MARCUS. What about my stocks?

KEVIN. CRASHED.

MARCUS & DIANE. Shit!

SCENE NINE – Stuart Needs His Joke Book Now

(**STUART**, **JACK**, *and* **BRIE** *enter.* **BRIE** *carries a half completed puppet.*)

STUART. Marcus! Diane! Pay attention. There's forty minutes until showtime. Brie needs to dry off her soggy puppets, and Jack still can't find my joke book! A word of advice, Jack, if you want to be more than just our little intern with a big brain, you need to be more responsible!

(*to* **MARCUS** *and* **DIANE**)

Have you two practiced your salsa yet?

DIANE. Forget the salsa!!

MARCUS. I can't work with this!

STUART. Hey there, compadres! It's just nerves! Shake it out! You'll feel better.

DIANE. I feel sick.

MARCUS. Great. I'd rather do a solo.

DIANE. Use your left hand. Feels like someone else.

STUART. Come on, team! We are running out of time! Without my jokebook, I'm up the creek without a punchline!

BRIE. Stuart, why don't you just wing your stand-up routine?

STUART. Because I can't...Even since I told that joke on the boat cruise about the "Paraplegic at sea", Jerry from HR –

(**STUART** *points up to the booth.*)

– I know you're listening, Jerry – he makes me censor all my material. Look, I know there's no joy in Chimeville right now. But I'm sure if we just make it work, everything will be fine!

SCENE TEN – The CEO Is Here

(Suddenly, a loud noise comes over the speakers and the lights flicker. The CEO's booming voice is heard.)

VOICE OF CEO. Stuart!

STUART. He's here!

JACK. The Phantom!

BRIE. Wrong theatre.

STUART. It's the CEO! Sir, what an honour to have you join us for our little talent show.

VOICE OF CEO. Stuart, I gave you a chance to fix your branch and this is what you do? Throw some pansy little love-in?

STUART. A love-in! That's a good one, sir. No, this is certainly not one of those 'hippie' love-ins…we're definitely not sitting around in a circle, smoking the dope…which is illegal! And wrong. Unless it's medicinal. I understand it's good for nausea. Like when you're pregnant. I mean, you shouldn't smoke pot when you're pregnant! That's just silly. And insulting. To all the expectant mothers that will be here tonight. Like Mary-Anne from Accounts Payable – oh, she's good and pregnant. She's not? Hunh.

VOICE OF CEO. Stuart, what the hell are you talking about?

STUART. The talent show team builder. I wish you could have seen the opening number!

VOICE OF CEO. I did. In fact, I'm watching you right now. I had Kevin from IT set up a live feed to my office.

(The LCD screens show a live shot of the stage.)

But I'm too busy to babysit you. I've got work to do and a manicure in minutes! Now, Stuart, sales at the Toronto branch are down forty percent!

STUART. Really that much? Wow. Who's in charge of that?

VOICE OF CEO. You are!

STUART. *(realization)* I am? Well of course I am!

VOICE OF CEO. Your employees are chasing the same leads, your departments aren't communicating, and the only thing you care about is your office's fantasy hockey league!

STUART. Well, when you put it that way – yeah, that's not good. But I am committed to leading our branch through this dark time.

VOICE OF CEO. There is only one way to get your team to work together. Do you know what that is?

STUART. Positive reinforcement?

VOICE OF CEO. Positive reinforcement? Don't make me laugh. I mean it – don't. Competition is the only means of getting an excellent performance from your employees! Make them fight for your approval! Then fire the weakest link – just like Enron.

JACK. Probably not the best example.

STUART. Sir, I believe our office woes stem from poor morale. If I can inspire everyone with this show, then firing someone won't be necessary!

VOICE OF CEO. Stuart your naivety amuses me. And I hate being amused. Therefore, to prove how stupid you are, I give you this one chance. But when you fail, and you will fail, you'll fire someone on this stage tonight.

JACK. One of us?

BRIE. But we were picked randomly from the talent hat!

VOICE OF CEO. Shut up!

Stuart, I'll make this easy for you. Fire the morale problem. Do you understand me?

STUART. Yes sir. Thank you, sir.

VOICE OF CEO. Thanks is a dirty word.

(The **CEO** *disappears.)*

SCENE ELEVEN – Stuart Tries To Keep It Together

JACK. Fired? This is the only job I've ever liked!

DIANE. I clawed my way to the top. I need this job!

BRIE. I have a student loan!

MARCUS. I can't get fired! I'm being groomed for corporate!

STUART. Everyone, listen up. In times of crisis, we must do as the penguins do. Come together and sing. Felix, some thinking music!

SONG – "WE CAN KEEP IT TOGETHER"

STUART.

THERE'S A DEADLINE COMING AND IT ALL LOOKS BLEAK

AND THE MAN HAS GOT YOU RUNNING AND NO ONE WILL LET YOU SPEAK

DON'T YOU FROWN

DON'T YOU LET IT GET YOU DOWN

THERE'S A BRIGHT LIGHT SHINING AT THE END OF THE WEEK

YEAH THE CEO IS MAD, BUT I'M THE DAD

NOTHING BAD'S GONNA HAPPEN WHILE I STILL STAND

SO CHIN UP, GET UP, AND HAVE A LITTLE FAITH

CAUSE IT'S ALL GONNA BE OKAY

HOW WE GONNA DO IT?

HOW AM I TO KNOW?

BUT LET'S DO THINGS FAST AND LET'S THINK THINGS SLOW

LET'S PLAY OUT EVERY ANGLE AND MEASURE EVERY CURVE

WE COULD SPEND OUR TIME DEBATING

BUT WHAT WOULD THAT SERVE?

DO WHAT I SAY AND NOT WHAT I DO

AND DO IT FAST BECAUSE WE'RE RUNNING OUT OF TIME

I'VE HAD WAY TOO MUCH COFFEE

AND TO PULL THIS THING OFF

WE'RE GONNA NEED A LITTLE MUSIC AND RHYME

I KNOW IT'S BUSINESS AND WORK
AND WORK'S NOT SUPPOSED TO BE FUN
BUT CALL ME D'ARTAGNAN, MY MUSKETEERS,
ONE FOR ALL AND ALL FOR ONE!

WE CAN KEEP IT TOGETHER
I BELIEVE IN YOU, SAY YOU BELIEVE IN ME YEAH
WE CAN KEEP IT TOGETHER
AND WE ALL KNOW THAT IT'S ALL ABOUT THE TEAM
Come on, guys, join in! Let's band together. We need
to settle down and focus.
THINK! HAVE I EVER YOU LET DOWN?

ALL.

NO.

STUART.

OR SCREWED AROUND?

ALL.

NO.

STUART.

OR BEEN TOTAL CLOWN?

ALL.

WELL..

STUART.

DON'T ANSWER THAT
WE NEED SOME TEAM MORALE AND THAT'S WHAT'S
WE'RE GONNA GET
NOW LET'S HEAR SOME GOOD IDEAS

BRIE.

SIR?

STUART.

YES MY LITTLE PET?

BRIE.

MAYBE WE SHOULD STICK TO THE PLAN

STUART.

WHAT PLAN?

JACK.

THE SHOW, STUART.

STUART.

RIGHT – THE SHOW! ON WITH THE SHOW!

MARCUS.

THIS IS NEVER GONNA WORK

DIANE.

FOR ONCE WE AGREE

STUART.

WHAT WAS THAT?

MARCUS.

NOTHING SIR

DIANE.

JUST TALKING STRATEGY

STUART.

I KNOW IT SEEMS OUT OF REACH
BUT TRUST ME IT'S ABOUT TO BEGIN
SO JOIN ME NOW IN SINGING LOUD
AND LET ME HEAR YOU SING TO WIN

WE CAN KEEP IT TOGETHER

ALL.

WE CAN KEEP IT TOGETHER

STUART.

I BELIEVE IN YOU

ALL.

AND I BELIEVE IN ME

STUART.

YEAH! WE CAN KEEP IT TOGETHER

ALL.

AND WE ALL KNOW THAT IT'S ALL ABOUT THE TEAM

STUART.

YOUR DAY IS HARD AND LONG I ADMIT IT
BUT DON'T YOU LET IT GET YOU DOWN

ALL.

NO NO NO NO

STUART.

JUST KEEP THAT STICK ON THE ICE

NEVER QUIT IT
IT'S ALL GONNA TURN AROUND

ALL.

WE CAN KEEP IT TOGETHER
I BELIEVE IN YOU
AND I BELIEVE IN ME
WE CAN KEEP IT TOGETHER
AND WE ALL KNOW THAT IT'S ALL ABOUT THE TEAM

WE CAN KEEP IT TOGETHER
AND WE ALL KNOW THAT IT'S ALL ABOUT THE
NEVER STOPPING, NEVER DOUBT
THE CHIME CANADA TEAM!

STUART. Alright, team! I knew we were on the same page! Marcus and Diane, let's get you into those costume!

MARCUS. Let's just do this fast.

DIANE. With your reputation, that's a guarantee.

STUART. Come on, guys! Turn that frown upside down. We can keep it together…

(**STUART**, **MARCUS** *and* **DIANE** *exit.*)

SCENE TWELVE – Match Of All Matches

BRIE. This is terrible! One of them might get fired!

JACK. Shouldn't you be worried more about us?

BRIE. Come on Jack! We're no morale problem! We get along so well –

JACK. As friends.

BRIE. As friends.

JACK. Exactly.

BRIE. Right.

JACK. Yah! If only we could get them to like each other the way we like each other...
As friends!

BRIE. As friends!

BRIE. Totally.

JACK. For sure.

BRIE. That's it! We can fix this.

JACK. How?

BRIE. All we have to do is get Marcus and Diane to like each other.

JACK. You may need to flesh that out a bit more.

BRIE. We'll plant our seed in them.

JACK. Ew.

BRIE. Think about it! I know everything about everyone, right? And you, well, and you know everything about everything! We'll use the hectic atmosphere of the show to make the match of all matches. Marcus and Diane.

JACK. Great! And I know exactly how to do it!

BRIE. How?

JACK. It's a simple system, really. First we analyze a mash-up of relevant personal data into an alpha version of the system, which we throw into a regression analysis, followed by a zero-sum equation to determine the single common variable.

BRIE. Great!

(She turns away from him.)

Meanwhile, I'll start a sexy rumour.

JACK. We work so well together…

BRIE. As friends!

JACK. As friends!

*(**STUART** enters.)*

STUART. *(with cue cards)* I think I got that testy twosome under control, so clear the stage, clear the stage before they change their minds.

*(**JACK** and **BRIE** exit.)*

So up next we have Marcus and Diane with a spicy salsa! Those are some nice taquitos!

(LCD: HOSTILE WORKPLACE LANGUAGE!)

Breasts.

(LCD: ACCEPTABLE WORKPLACE LANGUAGE!)

*(**STUART** exits.)*

SCENE THIRTEEN – Stratango

(**MARCUS** *dances onstage. He is dressed in sparkled pants and an open vest. He stands proudly at centre.* **DIANE** *enters and walks straight to* **MARCUS**. *She is wearing a brightly coloured polka dot dress, complimented nicely by the massive fruit hat on her head.*)

DIANE. I hate you for this.

MARCUS. It looks good.

DIANE. It looks like Havana threw up on me.

MARCUS. Felix, give us some spice!

(**FELIX** *starts a salsa beat.* **MARCUS** *steps on* **DIANE**'s *toe.*)

DIANE. Watch it!

MARCUS. Shut up! We need to talk. I can't get fired!

DIANE. No shit! Neither can I! What the hell are we going to do?

MARCUS. I've been here eight years! Why can't those little laptop lovebirds get fired?

DIANE. Jack and Brie? Not a chance. Unless…

MARCUS. What? What?!

DIANE. Marcus, we need to turn them against each other.

MARCUS. What, like, start a fight?

DIANE. You got it.

MARCUS. So they become the morale problem.

DIANE. And not us.

MARCUS. But we can't work together.

DIANE. Which why we need to work together…

MARCUS. Ugh.

DIANE. Ugh.

MARCUS. But they're so…likable. What could we use against them?

(*Suddenly, a puppet comes from on stage from the wings.* **BRIE** *runs on.*)

BRIE. Jack, stop! Don't throw it! Sorry, guys, we were just fixing these for the puppet show.

(**JACK** *enters with a puppet.*)

JACK. You guys look great!

(*He imitates the theme song:*)

So you think you can dance dance dance...

BRIE. Do your Cat Deeley impression!

JACK. *(as the one and only Cat Deeley)* I'm Cat Deeley! Here are your....

JACK & BRIE. *(imitating)* Judges!

(**STUART** *enters.*)

STUART. Guys, you're interrupting their steamy salsa!

(*LCD: HOSTILE WORKPLACE LANGUAGE!*)

Uh, not steamy – carnal (!) moist (!) temperate? Get offstage.

(**JACK** *and* **BRIE** *exit.*)

Gosh, it's so hard to get kids these days to take things seriously!

(**STUART** *looks at* **DIANE** *and laughs heartily at her as he exits. The salsa resumes.*)

DIANE. The wheels are turning for me.

MARCUS. I can see the smoke.

DIANE. You're an ass. We have to use what we know.

MARCUS. Talk your marketing magic.

DIANE. Kevin, PowerPoint me!

(*A Presentation cues up on the LCDs.*)

Brie's demographic profile. She's single. She claims independence but is completely preoccupied with finding Mr. Right. She watches *Sex in the City* reruns and buys only yellow label No Name food products. Disgusting.

MARCUS. Perfect. Not a lot of lead-time, but we're selling solutions here and that's where I'm top of my game. Now, while I do Brie, you do Jack.

DIANE. Wait, no. I can't do that. I do the data, Marcus. I don't close the deal.

MARCUS. You're wasting time, Diane.

DIANE. Oh shut up and teach me then. Kevin!

MARCUS. What's Jack's stats?

DIANE. Jack's demographic profile. He's a geek. His only girlfriend was virtual. He's intelligent, socially awkward and impressionable – a marketer's dream – he'll buy anything if it makes him feel cool.

MARCUS. That's the key. Remember: Use your body, not your brains.

DIANE. That's it? Easy.

MARCUS. Like Sunday morning.

DIANE. Then it's settled. Marcus, go close the deal with Brie.

MARCUS. I'm on her. It. I'm on it.

(**DIANE** *and* **MARCUS** *exit.*)

SCENE FOURTEEN – Something Must Be Done

(JACK and BRIE enter after they leave.)

BRIE. Look! They're already working together! This is going to be so easy. High five!

(STUART enters in a panic.)

STUART. Brie! Why aren't you answering your phone? You are our Director of First Impressions and my first impression is that you aren't answering your phone! I'm sorry. It's just that Tony from Maintenance just told me my fly has been down this whole time. Why didn't you say something?! I'm not wearing underwear. Cathy locked me out of the house last night because I was spending too much time at work so I had to sleep in the wood shed and then my daughter called me on my cell at 2 AM from school because she was broke and I think a little drunk. So I woke up with a crick in my neck and a squirrel on my head and no fresh underwear and I still can't find my joke book and now Marcus and Diane are about to kill each other! Oh god, I can't feel my left arm. It's starting – burnt toast! I smell burnt toast! Burnt toast! Can anyone else smell burnt toast? Am I the only one –

BRIE. Stuart, Stuart, Stuart! Calm down, Stuart. It's just cause Marcus and Diane are Sales and Marketing.

JACK. The rage, the hatred. It's in their blood.

BRIE. Their food fight at the spring BBQ?

JACK. Cost a ton in Blackberry repairs!

STUART. You're right! Something must be done! Well don't just stand there, do something!

BRIE. You know what I think? I think it's a thin line between love and hate. You get me?

STUART. *(thinking for a moment)* Hmmmm…no.

BRIE. I think Diane is lonely.

STUART. A lonely, frightened deer caught in a trap…

JACK. She's more like the trap than the deer.

BRIE. Jack!

> (*to* **STUART**)

> It's funny because I thought she and Marcus had a thing once.

STUART. Really? A thing? What kind of thing? A sexual thing?

BRIE. I remember Marcus saying one of Diane's presentations was "sexy."

STUART. Sexy?

JACK. Yeah! Marcus was really into her charts and graphs.

STUART. Well, well, well! I think they had a little tickle under the table.

BRIE. Ha, ha. A secretive snuggle in the sick room?

JACK. Some lunchtime liaisons in the coffee lounge?

STUART. Some wild office sex, with her bent over that oak desk in the storage room, wearing nothing but stockings and a lab coat.

JACK & BRIE. Exactly.

STUART. Well, that is very interesting information.

BRIE. It's probably nothing.

STUART. Nothing is nothing. When you grow up, you'll begin to truly grasp that concept. Okay, sharks! Let's keep swimming!

JACK. Wait! What are we doing?

STUART. Brie, you need to WetVac your puppets. Jack, you need to find my jokebook. And I need to go to the little boys room. Break!

> (**JACK, BRIE** *and* **STUART** *exit.* **MARCUS** *enters, tries to get* **BRIE***'s attention but fails.*)

SCENE FIFTEEN – Marcus Can't Close the Deal

MARCUS. Brie – ! Ugh! It's okay. I can do this. I can do this. I'm good. I'm hot. I'm – what the hell am I doing…?

SONG – "THE SALES GUY"

MARCUS.
I'M SUPPOSED TO BE,
THE KINDA GUY YOU SEE,
STRUTTIN' UP BAY AND KING
I'M POURED INTO MY SUITS
I COLOURIZE MY ROOTS
THE GIRLS I DATE ARE COVERED IN BLING
BUT WHEN PEOPLE GET TO KNOW ME
I INSTANTLY GET LONELY
I NEVER MAKE AN HONEST CONNECTION
AND SOME PEOPLE HERE AT WORK,
THEY THINK THAT I'M A JERK
BUT WHEN I TAKE A CLOSER INSPECTION

THERE'S AN AWFUL LOT OF THINGS THAT I DON'T KNOW
AND I MISSED MY CHANCE SOME TIME AGO
TO BE REAL LEADER AND DO WHAT THEY DO
THE PROBLEM IS I HAVE NO EQ
I CARRY MY WEIGHT
I HOLD MY HEAD HIGH
BUT I'M SIMPLY NOT A SALES GUY

AND NOW I GOT THIS TASK
IT'S AN AWFUL LOT TO ASK
FROM SOMEONE WHO IS FINDING IT HARD
TO JUST KEEP SELLING WITH A SMILE
WHEN REALLY ALL THE WHILE
I'M TERRIFIED OF LOSING MY GUARD
BUT IT'S TIME FOR THAT TO END
I KNOW I CAN TRANSCEND
I HAVE A CERTAIN DEADLINE APPROACHING
AND WITH NO ONE ELSE AROUND
I GOTTA STAND MY GROUND

AND GIVE MYSELF SOME MUCH NEEDED COACHING

YOU CAN BE ANYTHING IF YOU JUST TRY
NOT WAIT AROUND ASKING WHEN OR WHY
A WOLF MAKES MANY ENEMIES AND A SHEEP WILL
TRY TO WIN FRIENDS AND INFLUENCE PEOPLE
THROW ROUND SOME WEIGHT
HOLD YOUR HEAD HIGH
AND TRY AND BE A SALES GUY

WHY, COULDN'T I BE WHAT MY MOTHER
ALWAYS EXPECTED I BE
MARCUS, THE FANCY LAWYER
OR MARCUS. M.D
NO I'M NOT SOME DISAPPOINTMENT
I REALLY DO GIVE A DAMN
AND IT'S TIME I STOPPED ACTING LIKE A LITTLE BOY
AND BECAME A MAN

I COULD BE THE GUY WHO DEFIES TRADITION
WHO'S KNOWN ROUND THE BUILDING FOR EARNING
COMMISSION
ALWAYS BEING TOASTED AT THE BAR
ALWAYS COMING IN WAY UNDER PAR
I'LL CARRY MY WEIGHT
I'LL HOLD MY HEAD HIGH
AND I CAN BE THE SALES GUY, IF I TRY
I CAN BE THE SALES GUY
I CAN BE THE SALES GUY
I CAN BE THE SALES GUY

SCENE SIXTEEN – Marcus Welcome Brie

(**MARCUS** *takes a few breaths to steady himself.* **BRIE** *enters.*)

BRIE. Hey Marcus, have you seen Jack? We need to work on our puppet show but Cindy the Printer Poodle isn't finished yet. We've had to replace the colour cartridge! Story of my life!

MARCUS. Hahaha! Brie, you are so funny. I am glad we're friends. A good friend is what you need right now.

BRIE. What do you mean?

MARCUS. Nothing! I'm just saying – the word around the water cooler is that your friend Jack has been talking smack about you. Ugh! Men! Let's go grab a Pom-tini, talk about it —

BRIE. Wait. Marcus, there is no way Jack would do that. I'm going to go straighten this out –

MARCUS. Wait, wait wait. Oh Brie. I was trying to protect you, but you've tied my hands. You must know. Jack told Stuart you were the morale problem here at Chime. Cause you're always up in everyone's business, you know?

BRIE. He said that about me?

MARCUS. I know. It hurts. Come here, let me hold you.

BRIE. I don't believe it.

MARCUS. Brie! Brie. Listen to me. The bottom line is this: Jack and his career will always come first. You come second, if you come at all.

BRIE. You mean –

MARCUS. Yes. Jack doesn't want to drag around dead weight...

BRIE. Dead weight? He thinks I'm fat? He thinks I'm FAT!

SCENE SEVENTEEN –
Welcome to the Business with Marcus

SONG – "WELCOME TO THE BUSINESS"

MARCUS.
> ARE YOU FEELING FOOLISH?
> ARE YOU FEELING SCARED?
> ARE YOU FEELING NERVOUS?
> YOU FEELING UNPREPARED?
>
> ISN'T IT TRAGIC?
> AND AIN'T IT NICE
> THAT A PRETTY YOUNG THING LIKE YOU NEEDS MY
> ADVICE
> ARE YOU PISSED THE WOOL'S BEEN PULLED RIGHT
> OVER YOUR EYES
> I'M AFRAID, IN THIS GAME, THAT'S NO BIG SURPRISE

*(**STUART** enters, sees what is happening and then sneaks out.)*

> WELCOME TO THE BUSINESS GIRL
> IT'S HARD TO FIND YOUR PLACE
> PEOPLE CUT DEALS BEHIND YOUR BACK
> AND THEY LIE RIGHT TO YOUR FACE
> MAYBE YOU'LL BE A CEO ONE DAY
> BUT NOW YOU'RE ON THE BOTTOM RUNG
> IT'S A COLD, CONNIVING BUSINESS GIRL
> AND OOOH AIN'T IT FUN

*(**MARCUS** exits. **STUART** enters.)*

SCENE EIGHTEEN – Stuart Stirs the Pot

STUART. My little wedge of Brie! I see what you're trying to do, but getting up close and personal with Marcus isn't going to improve morale. Kudos for taking one for the team, though.

BRIE. What? No, I wasn't – hey, has Jack been talking to you?

STUART. Oh no, you found out! Somebody's a blabbermouth. Oh well! You'd better run along and get ready for your puppet show!

(**BRIE** *exits.* **JACK** *enters.*)

JACK. Stuart, I found your jokebook! It was in the executive washroom under your copy of The Secret!

STUART. Cosmic lesson learned.

JACK. Have you seen Brie?

STUART. Not since she was making out with Marcus –

JACK. What?

STUART. I know. What a trooper. I told her it wasn't necessary! Oh! The cat is out of the bag about your surprise guitar song for her. Not my fault! Now go get 'em, tiger!

(**STUART** *exits.* **DIANE** *enters.*)

SCENE NINETEEN – Diane Welcomes Jack

DIANE. Hey there, Jack Flash. I need you…

JACK. Huh?

DIANE. …in my division. There was an opening last week. Brie was supposed to give you a heads-up.

JACK. I didn't even know about it. She must have forgot.

DIANE. Women never forget. It's such a shame. We all knew you were perfect for the job. Even Brie vouched for you.

JACK. She did?

DIANE. She said that the data analyst job would keep you safe from embarrassing yourself because you'd only be working with numbers – not people. Safety in numbers, she said! Ha, ha – she's so funny.

JACK. But Brie's my friend. She wouldn't say that about me.

DIANE. Oh Jack. Big, strong, surly Jack. I know you think you're friends, but Brie is also "friends" every guy in the office – all funny and flirty. She doesn't see you like I do.

JACK. Are you saying she's been backstabbing me…backstabbing me behind my back? I can't believe this…

SCENE TWENTY –
Welcome to the Business with Diane

SONG – "WELCOME TO THE BUSINESS"

DIANE.

DON'T ACT SO SURPRISED KID
SHE'S A WOMAN AFTER ALL.
WHEN WE TELL YOU SOMETHING'S SPECIAL
WE PROBABLY MEAN IT'S SMALL.

YOU WANNA GET AHEAD JACK
TURN YOUR HEART TO STONE
IF YOU'RE GONNA GET AHEAD BOY
YOU DO IT ON YOUR OWN

SOME ARE BORN TO FOLLOW, SOME ARE BORN TO
LEAD
AND A PRETTY LITTLE PIECE OF ASS IS THE LAST
THING YOU NEED

WELCOME TO THE BUSINESS BOY
YOU'RE NOW A PART OF IT
SMILES, FROWNS, UPS AND DOWN
AND OFTEN FULL OF SHIT
MAYBE YOU'LL BE A CEO ONE DAY
BUT FOR NOW YOU'RE ON THE BOTTOM RUNG
IT'S A TERRIBLE, BRUTAL BUSINESS BOY
BETTER LEARN THAT WHILE YOU'RE YOUNG

SCENE TWENTY-ONE – Sweet Like Candy

(**BRIE** *enters.*)

BRIE. Jack Staple.

JACK. Brie Damillo.

BRIE. Damillio.

JACK. Damillio.

BRIE. I was looking for you.

JACK. I'm right here.

BRIE. Ha. Yes you are!

JACK. You're in a good mood.

BRIE. A wonderful mood.

JACK. I am happy that you're happy.

BRIE. Really?

JACK. Oh yes.

BRIE. Wonderful.

JACK. Glorious.

BRIE. Nifty!

JACK. Stupendous!

BRIE. Good times.

JACK. We are friends.

BRIE. Good friends.

JACK. Sharing a laugh.

(*They laugh awkwardly then turn away saying,*)

Bitch!

BRIE. Bastard!

JACK & BRIE.

IT'S HARD TO HANDLE
BUT IT HAPPENS EVERY DAY
FRIENDS DON'T SAY THE THINGS THEY MEAN
AND THEY DON'T MEAN THE THINGS THAT THEY SAY

MARCUS & DIANE.

BUT DON'T YOU WORRY
EVERYTHING WILL BE ALRIGHT

DIANE.

    ONE THING I'VE LEARNED

MARCUS.

    OVER THE YEARS I'VE LEARNED

BOTH.

    ONE THING I'VE LEARNED

ALL.

    DON'T GO DOWN WITH A FIGHT

    WELCOME TO THE BUSINESS
    YOU GOTTA GET PISSED IF YOU WANNA GET PAID

MARCUS & DIANE.

    SOMETIMES YOU SCREW

JACK & BRIE.

    SOMETIMES YOU'RE SCREWED

ALL.

    BUT NOBODY'S GETTING LAID

    MAYBE I'LL/YOU'LL BE A CEO ONE DAY
    BUT FOR NOW I/YOU GOTTA PAY WHAT'S DUE
    WELCOME TO THE BUSINESS
    AND THE BUSINESS WELCOMES YOU...YOU...YOU...
    YOU!

    (**JACK** *and* **BRIE** *storm off.*)

SCENE TWENTY-TWO – Stuart Brings Sexy Back

(**MARCUS** *approaches* **DIANE.**)

MARCUS. Well, I think we got the ball rolling.

DIANE. You finally did something useful. Guess I owe Janet from Customer Insights forty bucks.

(**STUART** *enters.*)

STUART. Let's keep this show on track! First the puppet show, then I'm up to the plate next with my grand slam stand-up routine! Got my A material back! What are you two doing?

DIANE. I was just clearing some things up with Marcus.

STUART. Oh. Oh I see. Personal things, I imagine?

(**STUART** *winks at* **DIANE.**)

DIANE. What was that?

STUART. Nothing.

DIANE. I saw you wink.

STUART. No, you didn't.

DIANE. You winked at me.

STUART. It was a tick. In my eye. Now, if you will excuse me, Marcus, I need to have a private conversation with Diane.

(*to* **DIANE**)

Psst!

DIANE. What is it?

STUART. I'm not going to beat around your bush.

DIANE. What? –

STUART. – It's about Marcus.

DIANE. Marcus?

STUART. I hear there's a certain head of marketing that Marcus finds sexy…

DIANE. What?…Really? Sexy? Did he say that – did he say sexy?

STUART. Irresistibly sexy.

(**DIANE** *looks at* **MARCUS**. **MARCUS** *is picking grapes off of* **DIANE***'s headpiece. He slightly chokes on one.* **DIANE** *looks back to* **STUART**.)

STUART. *(cont.) (mouthing it)* Irresistibly.

(**STUART** *exits.* **DIANE** *goes to* **MARCUS**.)

MARCUS. *(mouth full)* What was that?

DIANE. Nothing.

MARCUS. Man, this day has been wild! You know, Diane, I think that we're going to do it.

DIANE. Wh – what?

MARCUS. We are going to do it! Tonight!

DIANE. Huh?

MARCUS. Do it. You know, break up the little lovey doves, keep our jobs. Man, those guys don't stand a chance!

(**MARCUS** *exits.*)

DIANE. Right. Oh yes, of course. Do it. That. Do that. Yes, that is what we will do.

SCENE TWENTY-THREE – The Puppet Show

(**STUART** *enters.*)

STUART. Clear the stage!

(**DIANE** *exits in a hurry.*)

Time check!

(*The LCD reads: "23:58"*)

Oh Jiminy cricket! Let's keep this rehearsal rolling everybody! Okay, then I'll say: Ladies and gentlemen! Employees of Chime and your plus ones. I present to you an adorable puppet show by Jack and Brie! Take it away, kids!

(**JACK** *and* **BRIE** *enter.*)

BRIE. Welcome everyone! My name is Brie, and this is my friend Cindy the Printer Poodle. Say hi Cindy!

VOICE OF CINDY. Hi Brie!

JACK. And my name is Jack, and this is my good friend Bob the Stapler Dog.

VOICE OF BOB. Hello! What are we going to learn about today, Jack?

VOICE OF CINDY. I think that today we should learn about friendship.

BRIE. What a great idea!

VOICE OF BOB. I certainly know someone could learn a thing or two about being a friend.

VOICE OF CINDY. Zip it, you lousy stapler dog.

BRIE. Cindy, that's not very nice.

VOICE OF BOB. You know what they say, if you don't have anything nice to say, shut your goddamn mouth.

JACK. Now Bob, take it easy.

VOICE OF BOB. Say Jack, I'm confused!

JACK. Why are you confused, Bob?

VOICE OF BOB. Well, there two people over there. One. Two. Right?

JACK. Good, Bob! So what's the problem?

VOICE OF BOB. Well, all I see is one big fat sadistic floozie!

BRIE. Fat?!

VOICE OF CINDY. We're talking about friendship, Bob, remember? Let's look at Jack. Jack is what we call a bad friend. A bad friend is someone who is mean and selfish and hurts the people he's supposed to care about. Jack did that, didn't he, Brie?

VOICE OF BOB. Jack did not! Jack trusted Brie! Brie betrayed him!

VOICE OF CINDY. Brie did not! Jack walked all over Brie to climb the corporate ladder!

VOICE OF BOB. Brie likes to lie, doesn't she, Jack?

VOICE OF CINDY. You are heartless and despicable.

VOICE OF BOB. I'm gonna pop you one good, you vapid harlot.

VOICE OF CINDY. Bring it on, you scrawny little geek.

VOICE OF BOB. Oy! I almost forgot! Sticky Note Ned agrees with us.

BRIE. Who's Sticky Note Ned?

(**JACK** *reveals his left hand – with a sticky note on it.*)

STICKY NOTE NED. Three to two. You're outnumbered.

BRIE. This is ridiculous.

STICKY NOTE NED. You're ridiculous.

BRIE. Shut up Jack.

STICKY NOTE NED. You shut up.

(**BRIE** *snatches* **STICKY NOTE NED** *out of* **JACK**'s *hand and feeds it to* **CINDY**.)

JACK. You killed Sticky Note Ned!

BRIE. You'll be next. And your little dog too.

JACK. So career murder wasn't good enough for you? You had to resort to puppecide?

(**STUART** *enters.*)

BRIE. That's it! I'm out of here!

JACK. Me too!

STUART. I thought you had a 20 minute magic show too!

JACK AND BRIE. Screw you!

SCENE TWENTY-FOUR – The Aftermath

*(*JACK *and* BRIE *exit. The* CEO *appears.)*

VOICE OF CEO. STUART!!

STUART. Ah! Please don't surprise me like that, sir...

VOICE OF CEO. How is the rehearsal going, Stuart?

STUART. Great! Wonderful! Well, there was some delays due to the sprinkler accident, but as they say, it ain't over until the fat lady sings!

(The LCD BEEPS "HOSTILE WORKPLACE LAN-GUAGE" and after each of his attempts.)

And by fat lady, I mean obese lady (!)...overweight lady (!)...big boned (1)...A woman of substance?

VOICE OF CEO. Will you just shut up? When I come back, I want to see proof! Tangible results!

(The CEO *disappears.)*

STUART. Oh fiddlesticks. What am I gonna do? I need to run through my stand up routine, but I must deal with Jack and Brie! Okay, I'll do it real quick. Ahem...So, a blonde, a brunette and Jesus walk into a Japanese sushi bar in Gaytown during Ramadan –

(LCD: "HOSTILE WORKPLACE LANGUAGE" STUART *peers up at the booth.)*

Oh, come on, Jerry! It's just a sushi joke! It's a classic! I wish you knew what it felt like to have your art censored by a heartless HR jerk!

SCENE TWENTY-FIVE –
Stuart Help Jack with His Heart Song

(**JACK** *enters.*)

JACK. Stuart, I'm sorry, I should go…Brie hates me, and I think I hate her too, so I'm going to just call it a night –

STUART. Come here, my boy. I want to tell you a story. Visualize with me.

(**JACK** *closes his eyes.*)

It's just you and me here. Breathe in, breathe out. I want you to think of Chime as a metaphor for the human body. Tech Support is the legs, Marketing is the chest and pelvic region, and Management is the brain. Now, let's say that Head Office is a big machete, and that machete comes along and starts hacking at you. It hacks off your arms and one of your legs, and as you hop around helplessly, it grabs a meat tenderizer and starts going after your good foot like some sick game of whackamole. You look around and you are surrounded by the rotting mess of your own bloody dismemberment. As you try desperately to grab hold of a limb or ear, they slip from your finger-less palms, you are falling apart – literally – and you scream, 'What can we do? Oh, god, what can we do?'

WE CAN KEEP IT TOGETHER
I BELIEVE IN YOU
AND YOU BELIEVE IN ME, RIGHT?
WE CAN KEEP IT TOGETHER
COLLECT YOURSELF AND THE PIECES OF OUR TEAM

JACK. That was disturbing…yet poignant.

STUART. Yes. You need to write her that song, Jack. Come with me. I'll help you write your lyrics.

(**STUART** *and* **JACK** *exit.*)

SCENE TWENTY-SIX –
It Was Business, But Now It's Personal

(MARCUS enters.)

MARCUS. Kevin? Jerry? Thanks for keeping your mouth shut about me and Diane and our little scheme –

(DIANE enters.)

DIANE. Why, hello.

MARCUS. I was just talking about you.

DIANE. Oh, I see. Was it personal?

MARCUS. Well, um –

DIANE. Look, I've been thinking about our plan and something's come up suddenly.. It's got me all bothered…

SONG – "NOW IT'S PERSONAL"

DIANE. *(cont.)*

SOME PEOPLE CALL ME CRAZY
DON'T KNOW WHERE I'M COMING FROM
THEY THINK MY DAD WAS LAZY
OR THAT I HAD AN ALCOHOLIC MOM

I'M GOOD AT CLIMBING LADDERS
BUT I CLIMBED THEM ALL ALONE
WHEN YOU'RE GETTING SCREWED ALL DAY AT WORK
WHY GET IT WHEN YOU'RE AT HOME?

BUT I'M ATTRACTED TO TALENT
AND YOU'VE GOT MORE THAN ENOUGH
AND I KNOW YOU TAKE IT EASY
BUT WHEN THINGS GET ROUGH

YOU'RE GOOD TAKIN' CARE OF BUSINESS
I KNEW THAT BEFORE
BUT WATCHING YOU CLOSE CLOSE THE DEAL
I'M FEELING SOMETHING MORE
I'M GOOD, YOU'RE GOOD, WE'RE GOOD TOGETHER
BUT NOW THAT ISN'T ALL.
IT WAS BUSINESS NOW IT'S…PERSONAL

I KNOW I'M HARD TO HANDLE
TWO EX HUSBANDS WOULD AGREE
I'VE SEEN MY SHARE OF SCANDAL
BUT NEVER THOUGHT IT'D BE INVOLVING ME
I KNOW THIS ISN'T PROPER
WHAT I'M FEELING CAN'T BE RIGHT
BUT WHEN I'M SIZING UP YOUR OFFER
I'M FEELING JUST A LITTLE LESS TIGHT

BUT DON'T GET CRAZY IDEAS
I'VE SEEN BETTER THAN YOU
BUT UNLESS I'M LYING, THERE'S NO USE DENYING
THIS NEEDS NO THINKING THROUGH

YOU'RE GOOD AT TAKIN' CARE OF BUSINESS
I KNEW THAT BEFORE
BUT WATCHIN' YOU CLOSE THE DEAL
I'M FEELIN' SOMETHING MORE
I'M GOOD, YOU'RE GOOD, WE'RE GOOD TOGETHER
NOW THAT ISN'T ALL.
IT WAS BUSINESS NOW IT'S…PERSONAL

WHAT THE HELL IS WRONG WITH ME
I TOLD MYSELF THIS WOULD NEVER BE
IF I LOOKED AT MYSELF I'D SEE
SOMEONE I DON'T KNOW

I GUESS YOU HAVE THE RIGHT COMBINATION
OF LOOKS, CHARM, AND OCCUPATION
SO LET'S JUST STOP THIS ANTICIPATION
AND SEE WHERE THIS CAN GO…

OOH YOU'RE GOOD AT TAKIN' CARE OF BUSINESS
DID YOU KNOW BEFORE
THAT WATCHIN' YOU GO…
I'M FEELING SOMETHING…
I'M GOOD…YOU'RE GOOD…
NOW THAT ISN'T ALL.
IT WAS BUSINESS NOW IT'S…PERSONAL.

(**DIANE** *and* **MARCUS** *exit, clawing madly at each other.*)

SCENE TWENTY-SEVEN – Play It Again, JACK

(STUART and JACK enter.)

STUART. Are you ready?

JACK. Yeah. I'm a little nervous.

STUART. Don't worry so much. Just remember: keep it together.

JACK. But Brie still won't talk to me. She locked herself in her dressing room with a pint of Häagen-Dazs.

STUART. Oh, I've already taken care of that. I sent her a text message, told her her grandmother died. She'll be up any minute.

(BRIE rushes on stage.)

BRIE. Stuart! How did it happen?!

STUART. Good luck, son.

(STUART exits.)

BRIE. Stuart? Where are you going? What about my grandma!?

JACK. She's fine.

BRIE. What?

JACK. Stuart just needed to get his team back together.

BRIE. Yeah, well I'm sick of this team!

JACK. Didn't you used to believe in this show?

BRIE. I also used to believe in Santa Claus, the tooth fairy and the electric car.

JACK. Brie, listen! I don't know what went on tonight. But I want to say something. Stuart helped me re-write the lyrics to my song. Just hear me out! I think they really express how I feel.

SCENE TWENTY-EIGHT –
Bottom Line Attempt Number Two

*SONG – "BOTTOM LINE #2 OR LEPROSY LOVE
SONG"*

JACK.
YOU AND I FELL APART
LIKE WE HAD LEPROSY
SO LET'S RE-ATTACH OUR HEARTS
EVERY ARM, LEG AND KNEE
AND IF I'M WHAT YOU WANT
THEN LET'S JUST BE…
TOGETHER FOREVER
IN OUR BLOOD SPATTERED FANTASY

BRIE. That was a little strange.

JACK. It's a work in progress.

BRIE. Stuart helped you with those lyrics?

JACK. Yah, the part about the blood –

BRIE. Jack, he sleeps in his wood shed.

JACK. Gotcha.

BRIE. But I know what you're trying to say…and I agree.

JACK. So we're friends?

BRIE. Sure. Friends. But next time, you need to write your OWN lyrics, okay?

JACK. Okay.

BRIE. Okay.

JACK. You know, I really missed having you around…

BRIE. As a friend!

JACK. As a friend!

SCENE TWENTY-NINE – Time Is Up

(The CEO appears on the screens.)

VOICE OF CEO. TIME'S UP, STUART! …Who're you two?

JACK. I'm Jack Staple –

VOICE OF CEO. And I'm bored. Where is Stuart?!

(STUART sprints on stage.)

STUART. I'm here! I'm here!

JACK. That man is very rude.

STUART. Hush!! Sorry, sir, he's new. And from Turkey. His English isn't very good.

VOICE OF CEO. Get your team out here!

STUART. Marcus! Diane!

(DIANE and MARCUS enter. Their clothes are in disarray.)

VOICE OF CEO. Well, Stuart, where are my tangible results?

SCENE THIRTY –
Stuart Shows Us Some Highlights

STUART. Well, sir, I had Kevin from IT compile a highlights reel of our rehearsal – and it proves just how well our team has been working together tonight! Kevin, cue it up!

(The LCD screens show the title FUNNY BUSINESS – SEE WHAT WAS GOING ON. It is a compilation of clips from the rehearsal, roughly pasted together from different parts to give the impressions that **JACK**, **BRIE**, **STUART**, **DIANE** *and* **MARCUS** *were all backstabbing each other and saying terrible things about the others. The highlights reel ends with a doctored clip of* **MARCUS** *and* **BRIE** *that looks like they are making out. [SEE SCRIPT BELOW])*

(THE HIGHLIGHTS REEL script [shown on the LCD screens as a video]:)

STUART. Are you ready for some team building? Are you ready – are you ready – for some team building?

BRIE. I think Diane is –

JACK. – a big fat sadistic floozy.

BRIE. Marcus and Diane will get fired –

JACK. – Great! And I know exactly how to do it.

DIANE. Marcus, we need to turn Jack and Brie against each other –

MARCUS. – that's where I'm on top of my game –

DIANE. – you got it!

MARCUS. So while I do Brie, you do Jack.

DIANE. Easy.

MARCUS. Like sunday morning.

DIANE. Jack, I need you. I know you think you're friends, but Brie is friends with every guy in the office, all funny and flirty –

JACK. – are you saying she's been backstabbing me? Bitch! Bitch! Bitch!

BRIE. He said that about me? –

MARCUS. – Come here, let me hold you.

(A clip is shown of them almost kissing.)

DIANE. *(to* **JACK***)* There's an opening in my division.

JACK. Glorious.

(A clip of **JACK** *falling to knees in front of* **DIANE***, implicating a sexual act.)*

MARCUS. *(to* **BRIE***)* Bottom line, we are going to do it tonight.

BRIE. – Totally!

STUART. Wonderful! Head office will be so pleased.

(A clip is shown of **MARCUS** *and* **BRIE** *where* **MARCUS** *is moving behind* **BRIE***.)*

Big finish!

(The gyrating clip is looped, which looks like **MARCUS** *and* **BRIE** *are engaged in a sexual act. The highlights reel ends with "The End?" After a beat…)*

JACK. Brie!

DIANE. Marcus!

BRIE. Jack!

STUART. *(with innuendo)* Brie…

MARCUS. Diane!

BRIE. Stuart!

JACK. Marcus!

DIANE. Brie!

*(***FELIX** *plays a wrong note.)*

ALL. Felix!

JACK. Brie, what the hell was that?

BRIE. Me? What about you!

MARCUS. Diane, how could you!

DIANE. You are despicable!

THE CEO. Stuart, look at your team! I knew this pathetic patty-cake circle would fail. Stuart, pick one of them and fire them NOW!

STUART. Now?!

DIANE. Fire Marcus.

MARCUS. What?!

DIANE. He tried to sabotage the talent show. He lied to Brie about Jack! He's a liar!

MARCUS. You callous she-devil! Diane did it. Fire her. She preyed on Jack because she is evil!

DIANE. You lying piece of jackass!

JACK. Fire Brie! She set up Marcus and Diane, which is strictly against office romance policy! Right, Mr. CEO?

BRIE. Are you kidding? Fire Jack! All he does is…um…

(The **CAST** *all hum and ha about what* **JACK** *actually does.)*

JACK. Oh, come on!

STUART. Hold the phone! This was all…secrets and lies! Secrets and lies! Well, I'm very disappointed in all of you. But the good news is Jack and Brie, you don't have to hate each other, and Marcus and Diane, you don't have to like each other! Isn't that terrific?

JACK. My heart hurts.

BRIE. Oh play the violins, god!

JACK. I'm never going to play anything for you ever again.

BRIE. Good cause your song sucked.

JACK. I wrote it for you, and you suck, so do the math.

STUART. Come on guys!

DIANE. You got what you deserve.

MARCUS. You sold me out! Did the storage closet mean nothing to you?

DIANE. This is business, Marcus. You made that perfectly clear on the highlights reel!

SCENE THIRTY-ONE – We're All Hung Out To Dry

SONG – "HUNG OUT TO DRY"

MARCUS.
>THAT'S ALL YOU'VE GOT TO SAY FOR YOURSELF
>HARD TO BELIEVE WHAT I'M HEARING
>YOU'RE DONE WITH ME NOW I GO BACK ON THE
>SHELF
>WELL I AM NOT DISAPPEARING

DIANE.
>I GUESS I WAS STUPID TO EVER BELIEVE
>YOU COULD SOMEHOW EVOLVE
>BUT, LIKE ALL MEN, YOU LIE AND DECEIVE
>WELL YOU'RE NOT MY PROBLEM TO SOLVE
>
>IT WAS A WASTE OF TIME, THOUGH I DID TRY

MARCUS.
>HOW COULD YOU DO THIS TO ME AND LOOK ME IN
>THE EYE

DIANE.
>I COVERED MY ASS

MARCUS.
>AND ALL YOU HAD TO DO WAS LIE

BOTH.
>YOU GAVE ME NO CHOICE
>YOU HUNG ME OUT TO DRY

STUART. Everyone, get a hold of yourselves! We've got four minutes until the audience walks through that door! Jack, come on, tell Brie how you really feel and end this!

JACK. You are a no good hussy.

STUART. No, no, that is not it!

BRIE.
>I CAN'T BELIEVE THAT YOU'D SELL ME OUT
>AFTER ALL WE'VE BEEN THROUGH
>BUT I AM STRONGER, AND I HAVE NO DOUBT
>THE ONLY ONE SCREWED HERE IS YOU

JACK.

YOU SET ME UP, RIGHT FROM THE START
I GUESS I'M JUST FOOLISH AND YOUNG
YOU'RE SUCH A...I MEAN YOU'RE A...

BRIE.

WHAT'S WRONG JACK? CAT GOT YOUR TONGUE?

JACK.

NO YOU'RE JUST BITCHY, AND EVIL, AND DUMB!
DON'T TRY TO DEFEND, DON'T TRY TO DENY

BRIE.

YOU'VE TOTALLY CHANGED, AND I DON'T KNOW
WHY

JACK.

WELL I GUESS THAT'S THAT

BRIE.

I GUESS THAT'S GOODBYE

BOTH.

WHAT DID YOU EXPECT?
YOU HUNG ME OUT TO DRY

STUART. My team – my family – please! We can do this...

We can –
– KEEP IT TOGETHER
I BELIEVE IN YOU

ALL.

WELCOME TO THE BUSINESS

STUART.

WE CAN KEEP IT TOGETHER
WHAT ABOUT THE TEAM

ALL.

WHAT ABOUT THE TEAM?

STUART.

WE CAN KEEP IT TOGETHER

DIANE.

IT WAS BUSINESS, NOW IT'S PERSONAL

MARCUS.

I'M...THE SALES GUY...

STUART.

WE CAN KEEP IT TOGETHER

JACK.

MY DUAL CORE, NO MORE, SAY GOODBYE TO THE
BLOOD SPATTERED FANTASY

BRIE.

I NEED A GUY, JUST LIKE JUST LIKE JACK, THINKS I'M
FAT!

STUART.

WE CAN KEEP IT TOGETHER

ALL.

WHAT ABOUT THE TEAM
WHAT ABOUT THE TEAM
WHAT ABOUT THE TEAM?

STUART. I can't take it anymore! You're all so negative!
Fine, you wanna fight? I'll make ya fight! We're going
to battle this out the old-fashioned way. Every man for
himself. Forget team building. Forget this stupid talent
show. We're going to have a competition. A cockfight!
I'm gonna make you sing, and dance, and do office
things! And then, yes, someone will be fired! Do you
hear me? Fired!

THE CEO. I hear you loud and clear, Stuart, and I love this
bloodthirsty side of you. When the audience gets here,
they will act as judge and jury!

STUART. It's brilliant! Perfect! Now shake hands. Shake
hands, dammit!!

JACK & MARCUS.

IF IT'S A FIGHT YOU WANT A FIGHT YOU WILL GET

BRIE & DIANE.

COMING FROM YOU THAT IS HARDLY A THREAT
SO TRY NOT TO CHOKE

JACK & MARCUS.

AND TRY NOT TO CRY

ALL.

AS WE HANG YOU OUT

STUART. Game on!

ALL.

TO DRY!

(*The LCD counts down to 00:00*)

ACT II – THE COMPETITION

*(**STUART** enters while the house lights are still on.)*

SCENE ONE – Here We Show Team Spirit

STUART. Alright, everybody settle down…I SAID QUIET!

*(**STUART** calms himself.)*

Welcome Toronto branch of Chime Communications Canada. Now, I know you were all excited to see the Funny Business Talent Show Team Builder, but unfortunately we had to alter the evening's itinerary. Oh, but don't worry, you'll still be entertained. To make a long story short, I've been forced to make a redundancy. I thought this talent show would be the perfect way to motivate my team. But I learned that my team isn't all it's cracked up to be. So instead of seeing a tangy salsa, or a fluffy little puppet show, or my hilarious stand up routine, you will be witnessing an event that harkens back to ancient Rome. Bloodsport! A fight to save their jobs! And you will judge who gets the axe! YOU pick the loser! And by loser I mean victoriously challenged, Jerry! So, without further ado, I present your gladiators in the Funny Business Competition!

*(**BRIE** enters.)*

BRIE. Hi, I'm Brie. Remember that I know everything about everyone! I wouldn't want any of the incriminating things I've been privy to be leaked out…Right *Martha*? Just remember that when you're voting.

*(Lights up on **JACK**.)*

JACK. I'm Jack, and a logistic regression of the predicted binary categorical outcomes points clearly to my victory! And Brie sucks.

(Lights up on **MARCUS.** *)*

MARCUS. Hey, I'm Marcus. Emma, you're looking beautiful as always. Josh, love the new tie. Larry – is that your lovely wife or your daughter? Vote for Marcus. Because just imagine what this place would be like without me.

DIANE. Sanitary?

(Lights up on **DIANE.** *)*

I'm Diane. I'm here to win. I do my job and I do it well, so vote for me.

STUART. And I'm Stuart. I'm joined by my co-referee, our maestro from the mail room Felix. And no, Felix, you're not getting paid overtime, so deal with it. Anyhoo, as I said, you are our judges and your responses will be measured by our state of the art Applause-o-Meter. Kevin, please show us the Applause-o-Meter. Can I get some applause?

(The LCD shows APPLAUSE METER.)

As you can see, we've spared no expense. So make sure you make some noise for your favourite employee, or else they will be fired. Horribly, mercilessly fired.

And now for the first event! The first event will test our competitor's ability to think on their feet and test their humility. Each contestant must improvise a brief song describing the most embarrassing moment of their first day at work. The most humiliating story wins, as judged by you. You are singing for your lives. So make it hurt.

(music vamps)

SCENE TWO – It's My First Day

STUART. Brie, you're up first!

BRIE.

> MY FIRST DAY AT RECEPTION, DIDN'T GO VERY WELL
> I COULDN'T WORK THE PHONE, I SUCKED AT EXCEL
> I WAS CRYING AND ANGRY, SO I CALLED UP MY MOM
> BUT LITTLE DID I KNOW, I HAD PUSHED "INTERCOM"
>
> IT'S MY FIRST DAY, IT'S MY FIRST DAY
> TELL ME WHAT ELSE DO YOU WANT ME TO SAY
> SO SAY WHAT YOU NEED TO, THEN BE ON YOUR WAY
> VOTE BRIE! IT'S MY FIRST DAY!

STUART. She's throwing down the gauntlet, folks!

(LCD: BRIE'S APPLAUSE METER)

Not bad, not bad. Marcus, you're up next.

MARCUS.

> I WAS PROMISED AN OFFICE, I GOT A CUBICLE WALL.
> AND MY PARKING SPACE WAS ABOUT 3 FEET TO
> SMALL.
> WHEN I PULLED IN MY LEXUS, IT GOT THIS HUGE
> DENT
> AND LET'S JUST SAY I WAS INCONTINENT…
>
> IT'S MY FIRST DAY, IT'S MY FIRST DAY
> TELL ME WHAT ELSE DO YOU WANT ME TO SAY
> SO SAY WHAT YOU NEED TO , THEN BE ON YOUR WAY
> VOIE MARCUS! IT'S MY FIRST DAY!

STUART. Well, I'm uncomfortable. What about you folks?

(LCD: MARCUS' APPLAUSE METER)

That's pretty much what I thought too. Diane!

DIANE.

> I HAD THIS BIG CLIENT, WHO SAID I WAS FINE
> TO SELL HIS NEW STOCK OF CANADIAN WINE
> HE SAID GIVE ME A SLOGAN, I BLURTED RIGHT BACK
> "BIG BOSOM WINE, COME CHECK OUT MY RACK"
>
> IT'S MY FIRST DAY, IT'S MY FIRST DAY.

> WHAT THE HELL ELSE DO YOU WANT ME TO SAY
> SO SAY WHAT YOU NEED TO, THEN BE ON YOUR WAY,
> VOTE DIANE! IT'S MY FIRST DAY!

STUART. That was more dirty than embarassing but they seemed to like it!

> *(LCD: DIANE'S APPLAUSE METER)*

Last but not least…Jack.

> **(JACK** *is nervous to start. He gestures to have* **FELIX** *repeat the intro to his verse a few times while he prepares. Finally,* **DIANE** *pushes him out to centre stage.)*

JACK.

> I COULDN'T FIND THE BUILDING
> I WAS 2 HOURS LATE, I THREW UP AT LUNCH
> AND THAT REALLY SUCKED
> SOMEONE TAPED A SIGN ON MY BACK THAT SAID
> "GEEK"

DIANE.

> UH, JACK?

JACK.

> WHAT, DIANE?

DIANE.

> THAT JUST HAPPENED LAST WEEK

JACK.

> IT'S MY FIRST DAY, IT'S MY FIRST DAY
> TELL ME WHAT ELSE DO YOU WANT ME TO SAY
> SO SAY WHAT YOU NEED TO THEN BE ON YOUR WAY
> YOU'RE MEAN! IT'S MY FIRST DAY

> *(LCD: JACK'S APPLAUSE METER)*

STUART. And now the applause meter will tally the votes…

> *(LCD: THE WINNER IS JACK)*

SCENE THREE – Supply Room Blitz

STUART. And the winner is Jack! See, a lifetime of embarrassing moments finally paid off. Good for you, son. Next up, it's Supply Room Blitz! Ian from Day Care, will you please bring out the Supply Room Blitz loot bin! We all feel safer with Ian around. Thank you, Ian.

(NOTE: The following monologue is more of an improvisation for the actor playing **STUART.** *The original* **STUART** *worked with the writers for some material to use during this section. The actor playing* **STUART** *is free to use the improv from the original production below, or use it as a building block for their own take on it.)*

STUART. *(cont.)* Now I'd like to tell you a little bit about this part of the show. It's actually my favourite part because it's all about "stealing" office supplies or should I say borrowing things they'll never miss. Some say it's "wrong" or "illegal" but I feel it's more like something you have no need for yet feel entitled to. You know, like your appendix. Or Shoppers Optimum points or Paula Abdul on American Idol – I have no use for her but I sure like to have her there. Tonight is all about team building, you knowing sharing and caring. So I just want to ask you all straight out – show of hands – who here has stolen from our company? Oh yes, you have? Get out. Just kidding! I'm just being a chain yanker. I know this can be awkward because I'm the boss, you know quack quack quack. But I want to tell you that this is a safe room. You're all enveloped in Stuart's womb of secrecy. Which sounds icky, but it's a great place to be. Okay, I'll go first. Hmm.. Let's see…what has made it home in my briefcase over the years. Paper clips! I would bring them home for my daughter. She liked to make jewelry with them, you know bracelets and necklaces, the first time she went away to rehab – uh, camp! Hmm. What else. Pencils! For my morning Sodoku. Gosh, those are brain scramblers, aren't they? And I'm going to finish one of them one of these mornings, I know it. It's good to be goal oriented. Staples! I use them for shooting at the raccoons. I used to use the hose, but they say we have to conserve water so now I use the stapler. Nature first, that's my motto. Sticky notes! Oh, Jack here is our sticky note man. I've never seen someone use so many sticky notes! Every time I go to his cubicle, everything is just sticky. Well, I can feel the competition heating up and I know you can too. Enough of this witty banter! Let's play Supply Room Blitz! Now you will prove how business savvy you are by stealing as many office supplies as you can from the off stage cabinets. There's bonus points for taking the most Frequently Stolen Office Supplies, so keep your head on a swivel. Combatants, let's get ready to rumble! You have three minutes. Ready, set, steal!

(All madly dash offstage. **DIANE** *knees* **MARCUS** *in the groin as she exits.)*

MARCUS. Cheater!

*(***MARCUS*** *exits.* **BRIE** *trips* **JACK** *as she exits.* **DIANE** *enters with white out.)*

DIANE. *(pushing* **JACK** *out of the way)* Move it or lose it, office boy. White out! Frequently stolen item!

(LCD: White out 1000 pts.)

*(***DIANE*** *exits.* **MARCUS** *enters with pencils and blocks* **JACK**'s *path as* **JACK** *tries to exit again.)*

JACK. Marcus is cheating!

MARCUS. Stop being such a baby. Pencils!

(LCD: Pencils 1000 pts.)

JACK. Stuart!

STUART. Nobody likes a tattletale. Tick tock, tick tock.

*(***JACK*** *tries to dash offstage and nearly collides with* **BRIE**, *who enters with* **JACK**'s *guitar.)*

BRIE. Out of my way. I got a guitar!

JACK. That's mine!

STUART. Brie, that doesn't count. You can't steal from your coworkers, only your employers.

(**BRIE** *storms offstage.* **MARCUS** *enters with sticky notes.*)

MARCUS. I got stickies!

(**DIANE** *enters with sharpies.*)

DIANE. I got Sharpies here!

(*With both exits blocked,* **JACK** *is getting frustrated and confused.*)

STUART. Jack, stop fooling around!

JACK. I'm outta here!

(**JACK** *runs offstage through the house and out one of the theatre doors.* **DIANE** *and* **MARCUS** *toss their loot into the bin.*)

(*LCD: Sharpies 1200 pts.
Sticky Notes 2000 pts.*)

(**DIANE** *and* **MARCUS** *exit.* **BRIE** *enters with Bob the Stapler Dog.*)

BRIE. I got a stapler.

STUART. I'm afraid that doesn't count either.

BRIE. Why not?

STUART. Because it's a prop from the talent show. We already stole it from the supply closet.

(**BRIE** *angrily storms offstage again.* **DIANE** *enters with glue.*)

DIANE. I got glue!

(*LCD: Glue 1000 pts.*)

STUART. Diane, why do you only steal things you can inhale?

DIANE. Occupational hazard!

(**DIANE** *exits.* **BRIE** *enters empty-handed.*)

BRIE. Stuart, there's nothing left back there!

STUART. Well, you'd better hurry up! You're getting killed out here!

(As **BRIE** *exits, she runs into* **MARCUS** *who has a pair of scissors.)*

MARCUS. Don't even bother. These scissors were the last things back there.

*(***MARCUS** *makes a dash for the loot bin.)*

STUART. No running with scissors!

*(***MARCUS** *slows down, carefully placing the scissors in the loot bin.)*

(LCD: Scissors 1900 pts.)

BRIE. Stuart!!

STUART. Well, you'd better do something!

*(***BRIE** *exits through the theatre doors.)*

That's the spirit! Hey Kevin, where did Jack go? Do we have a live feed from outside the theatre?

(LCD: **JACK** *is shown creeping around the lobby of the theatre. He sneaks over to the bar, considers stealing a couple glasses, then eyes a clock on the wall. He looks around to make sure nobody is looking then snatches the clock off of the wall.)*

STUART. *(cont.)* Oh, looks like he's got himself a clock!

(As he is running away, he encounters **BRIE** *who tries to steal the clock from him.)*

Uh, oh. Looks like he's going to lose it.

(They get into an altercation, but **JACK** *is able to snatch the clock back from here and run away.)*

No, he's got it! Jack's got the clock!

*(***BRIE** *runs off in another direction.)*

Now, Kevin, what about Marcus and Diane? Where did they end up?

(LCD: We see a door backstage. There are loud banging noises from the other side of the door along with grunts and groans from **MARCUS** *and* **DIANE**. *We hear* **DIANE** *saying, "Give it to me,* **MARCUS**! *Give it to me!" The*

door opens to reveal **MARCUS** *and* **DIANE** *fighting over a three hole punch.)*

DIANE. *(ON SCREEN)* Give it to me, Marcus! I saw it first!

MARCUS. Finders keepers, losers weepers!

DIANE. I'm gonna kill you!

(LCD: They pause a moment. Suddenly they leap at each other in a passionate yet angry embrace as the door closes again.)

STUART. Ladies and gentlemen, the only question is: will he give her the three hole punch? We'll find out. Kevin, what about Brie? Where did Brie end up?

(LCD: We see a box office worker standing by a phone, helping a customer with tickets.)

Oh, that's Rachel from the box office. She's nice. Looks like they're very busy down there.

(Carefully, **BRIE** *sneaks up and tries to take the phone from her.)*

Looks like Brie is after that phone.

(LCD: **BRIE** *snatches the phone, but* **RACHEL** *notices.)*

RACHEL AT THE BOX OFFICE. Hey, you can't come back here! What are you –

(LCD: **RACHEL** *grabs the phone back from* **BRIE***, but they get into a scuffle.* **BRIE** *grabs* **RACHEL***'s hair, but* **RACHEL** *pushes her away and bashes* **BRIE***'s head against the desk. They wrestle to the floor.)*

STUART. This is turning into a smackdown!

(LCD: **RACHEL** *appears with the phone, but* **BRIE** *pulls her back down below the desk by her hair.* **BRIE** *pops up with the phone again.)*

Oh, looks like Brie's got the phone again!

(LCD: **RACHEL** *tackles* **BRIE** *to the floor again.)*

Nope, she's lost it.

(LCD: Two patrons, **DAN** *and* **FALK***, are standing in line watching this unfold.)*

FALK, A PATRON. Shouldn't we stop them?

(LCD: **DAN** *shakes his head "no." They lean in to get a better look. Finally,* **RACHEL** *climbs up to the desk. Her hair is a mess.* **BRIE** *follows, disheveled and defeated.)*

STUART. Why do I feel like I need a cigarette?

(LCD: **BRIE** *suddenly sees something off camera and dashes away.)*

Oh, I think Brie saw a hummingbird or a rainbow. Kevin, where has Jack got to?

(LCD: **JACK** *is shown sitting in the theatre lobby, holding his clock and drinking a soda.)*

Well, there's Jack! I suppose it doesn't occur to him he's in a race.

(LCD: **JACK** *suddenly looks down at his clock, realizes the time, and jumps up from his seat.)*

Kevin! How long do we have left?

(LCD: 20 seconds!)

Twenty seconds! Where the heck is everyone?!

*(***MARCUS** *runs onstage with the three hole punch.* **DIANE** *follows with a roll of toilet paper.)*

MARCUS. Three hole punch!

(LCD: Three hole punch 5000 pts.)

DIANE. That was low, Marcus.

(LCD: Toilet paper 50000 pts.)

*(***JACK** *suddenly bursts through the theatre doors and run on stage.)*

JACK. I got a clock! I got a clock!

(LCD: Clock 3 pts.)

MARCUS. Let's just get this over with! It's so obvious that I win! Come on, let's hear it for Marcus!

STUART. We still have – Kevin?

(LCD: 10 seconds!)

STUART. *(cont.)* Ten seconds! Where is Brie?

> (**BRIE** *enters from the theatre doors. She is dragging a heavy box.*)

There she is! What's she got there? Hurry up, Brie!

> (**BRIE** *drags the box up onto the stage.*)

A printer! She's got a printer!

> *(LCD: Printer 350000 pts.)*

MARCUS. No fair! She should be disqualified!

JACK. Stop being such a baby.

STUART. Who is the winner?

> *(LCD: The winner is Brie.)*

And the winner is Brie with 350000 pts! And Brie is quite right. The printer is the most frequently stolen item at the office. That's a good model, I have that one at home. Ian, for our Day Care, will you please clear the loot and loot bin! Let's hear it for Ian.

> (**IAN FROM DAY CARE** *drags the printer and loot bin offstage.*)

Nobody messes with Ian because he's quick on the draw with the time out. Now, for the final event, our competitors will be tested on the most important business skill: the ability to perform no matter how much you hate the people you work with. In this event Jack and Brie, and Marcus and Diane must prove that they can behave like professionals and check their egos at the door.

MARCUS. Wait, I have to be on the same team as her?

DIANE. Marcus is just going to drag me down

BRIE. Don't worry, Jack I won't let my ego get in the way.

JACK. I won't let my ego get in the way MORE!

STUART. Will you just shut up! Don't make me pull this show over. Each team will be given a topic, which they then must sell to you, the audience. Marcus and Diane, you're up first. Your task is to sell Toronto as a tourist destination.

DIANE. What?

MARCUS. Impossible!

STUART. That's right! On your marks…

BRIE. Haha, good luck suckers.

STUART. Get set…

JACK. You don't stand a chance.

STUART. GO!

SCENE FIVE – Tour the World in Toronto

(**JACK**, **BRIE** *and* **STUART** *exit.*)

DIANE. Marcus, I've got an idea. Keep up. Felix, improvise! Go, go, go!

SONG – "TOUR THE WORLD IN TORONTO"

DIANE. *(cont.)*
WHEN YOU'RE RUNNING SHORT ON DOUGH AND YOU GOT NOWHERE TO GO
YOU CAN TOUR THE WORLD, TOUR THE WORLD IN TORONTO
CHINA'S AT SPADINA AND QUEEN

MARCUS.
AND THE DANFORTH HAS SOME GREAT GREEK CUISINE

BOTH.
SO LETS TOUR THE WORLD, TOUR THE WORLD IN TORONTO
WHEN IT'S JULY 29 AND THE SUN AIN'T SHININ'
CAUSE YOU LIVE IN CANADA
REMEMBER YOU CAN GET HIGH AND WATCH THE RAINY SKY
AND IT AIN'T EVEN AGAINST THE LAW

DIANE.
WELL THE HOMELESS

MARCUS.
AND HOCKEY TEAM

BOTH.
SURE ARE A PROBLEM
BUT I'LL TAKE THE DEVIL I KNOW
LET'S TOUR THE WORLD
RIGHT HERE IN TORONTO

A CRUISE TO COZUMEL WOULD BE NICE I KNOW
BUT SCREW IT, IT COSTS WAY TOO MUCH TO GO
SO LET'S TOUR THE WORLD, RIGHT HERE IN TORONTO

(They conclude the song gasping for breath. They stare intensely at each other. **STUART** *enters.)*

STUART. I really didn't think you had it in you.

DIANE. Yes…your performance was…adequate.

MARCUS. Yes, and your plan was entirely…sufficient.

SCENE SIX – Musical As Team-Builder

STUART. And now for round two!

MARCUS. Oh yes, it's uh..their..turn.

DIANE. Marcus, we should go wait backstage.

MARCUS. What a great idea.

(They madly dash off stage.)

STUART. Okay! Jack and Brie!

*(**JACK** and **BRIE** enter.)*

You've got your work cut out for you! Your task is to pitch the idea of a corporate outing at a musical as a team building experience.

BRIE. What?

JACK. We already know that doesn't work!

STUART. An outing to a musical as a team building experience. You've got two minutes – starting now!

*(**STUART** exits.)*

BRIE. Uh –

JACK. Well?

BRIE. Well what?

JACK. Well, aren't you supposed to be good at this stuff?

BRIE. Uh, yeah. I'm great at creating proposals. That's why I work at reception. Aren't you supposed to be some kind of genius?

JACK. Not at this. Come on! Let's just think what tonight has been about. What's the theme? What's the bottom line?

BRIE. I don't know! God, I can't believe it. Marcus and Diane pulled it together and look at us. How are WE going to prove that an outing to a musical could be a team building experience?

JACK. I've got an idea…

*(**JACK** runs off stage to get his guitar.)*

SCENE SEVEN – Bottom Line Number Three

BRIE. Oh goody. Another song. Who wrote the lyrics this time?

JACK. Nobody. I mean…I don't have any yet.

BRIE. So what are you going to do?

JACK. Improvise. Like you said – speak from my heart.

(**JACK** *thinks for a moment, then begins playing.*)

SONG – "MY BOTTOM LINE"

I TALK TOO FAST
DON'T THINK THINGS THROUGH
I HAVEN'T ALWAYS BEEN GOOD TO YOU
BUT I'M HERE TO STAY COME RAIN OR SHINE
THAT'S MY BOTTOM LINE

I'M OFTEN SELFISH
I GET MY WAY
I'VE SAID SOME THINGS I DIDN'T MEAN TO SAY
BUT YOU'RE NOW A PART OF MY DESIGN
AND THAT'S MY BOTTOM LINE

LOOK AT THE MAN IN FRONT OF YOU
AND TELL HIM THAT HE DOESN'T CARE
TRY TO FORGET THOSE THINGS THAT HE SAID
WHEN HE FELT WORRIED OR SCARED

START TO SEE A DIFFERENT MAN
ONE WHO'LL BE AROUND
ONE WHO'LL KEEP YOUR HEAD IN THE CLOUDS
AND YOUR FEET ON THE GROUND

I TEND TO RAMBLE
WITH NO REASON OR RHYME
I'LL INVADE YOUR SPACE
I'LL SPEND YOUR TIME
BUT GIVE ME A CHANCE
THINGS WILL WORK OUT FINE
AND THAT'S MY BOTTOM LINE

Look at the man in front of you

BRIE.

I NEED A GUY

JACK.

HE'S GONNA BE AROUND

BRIE.

…JUST LIKE

BOTH.

I'M/HE'S GONNA KEEP YOUR/MY HEAD IN THE
CLOUDS
AND YOUR/MY FEET ON THE GROUND

JACK.

I'M STUBBORN AND SELFISH

BRIE.

I'M STUPID AND FRAIL

JACK.

I'M AFRAID TO SUCCEED

BRIE.

I'M AFRAID TO FAIL

BOTH.

YOU DON'T NEED TO BE BETTER
YOU JUST NEED TO BE MINE
CAUSE I LOVE YOU
AND THAT'S MY BOTTOM LINE

*(We see the Applause-o-Meter, which is orgasmically exploding with audience applause. **STUART** enters during the applause.)*

SCENE EIGHT – The Shit Hits the Fan

STUART. That was it! You two nailed it on the head! That's the perfect way to make a musical outing a team building experience! The classic love ballad!

BRIE. Jack…that was beautiful.

JACK. I wrote it for you and you're beautiful, so do the math.

STUART. Oh, this is almost too much for me. It swells the heart. Marcus and Diane!

(MARCUS and DIANE enter, clothes in disarray.)

DIANE. Yes sir! We were just…

MARCUS. Getting to yes.

STUART. That sounds productive.

(The CEO appears on the LCD Screens.)

VOICE OF CEO. Stuart! Why haven't you fired someone yet?

STUART. Oh, sir, I was just about to but then Jack sang this beautiful song, and Brie fell in love with him, and then Marcus and Diane had sex. Isn't that wonderful?

VOICE OF CEO. Touching. But you still failed. I told you to fire someone!

STUART. Yes, I know, sir. But I'd really like to say something.

(FELIX starts underscoring with a slow, pretty version of "WE CAN KEEP IT TOGETHER.")

All night, I've been this broken record saying, "Keep it together!" Meanwhile I was falling apart. The more I tried to fix things the worse they got. If anybody was causing morale problems, it was me and I'm sorry.

VOICE OF CEO. I understand, Stuart.

STUART. You do?

VOICE OF CEO. Yes. You're fired!

STUART. What!? But sir – I – I love this job. I need my team. Please – don't fire me.

BRIE. Sir, you can't do this!

VOICE OF CEO. I can do whatever I want! I run this company! I AM this company!

SCENE TEN – You Can't Fire Me

SONG – "YOU CAN'T FIRE ME I QUIT"

STUART.
YOU CAN'T FIRE ME

VOICE OF CEO. Yes I can.

STUART.
YOU CAN'T FIRE ME

VOICE OF CEO. Clean out your desk.

STUART.
YOU CAN'T FIRE ME

VOICE OF CEO. And get those ridiculous bumper stickers off the company car!

STUART.
YOU CAN'T FIRE ME

VOICE OF CEO. You've failed, Stuart.

STUART.
YOU CAN'T FIRE ME

VOICE OF CEO. Face it!

STUART.
YOU CAN'T FIRE ME...I QUIT.

JACK. Stuart, no...

BRIE. What about your severance package?

VOICE OF CEO. Oh please. Don't make me fire you too.

JACK. Wait! You can't do that!

BRIE. Firing us doesn't fix anything!

JACK. Stuart is like a father to me – a frequently inappropriate and embarrassing father, but a good one nonetheless! If you fire him... I quit!

BRIE. Me too!
YOU CAN'T FIRE ME

JACK.
YOU CAN'T FIRE ME

BOTH.
YOU CAN'T FIRE ME
I QUIT
YOU CAN'T FIRE ME

JACK.
YOU CAN'T FIRE ME

BOTH.
YOU CAN'T FIRE ME!
I QUIT!

VOICE OF CEO. I don't care! You two bottom feeders are replaceable. I can rebuild the office around Marcus and Diane.

DIANE. You mean…I'd be the general manager?

MARCUS. And I could work directly underneath her?

VOICE OF CEO. Yes! You could have it all. A company car, a corner office, a competitive salary…plus dental.

BRIE. Wait! Don't be tempted by a comprehensive dental plan!

JACK. Think of all the things that you've discovered about yourselves tonight!

MARCUS. I discovered a partner.

DIANE. And I discovered my erogenous zones.

MARCUS. You mean – the storage closet?

DIANE. The best four and half minutes of my life.

MARCUS.
YOU CAN'T FIRE ME…

VOICE OF CEO. I'm not.

DIANE.
YOU CAN'T FIRE ME!

VOICE OF CEO. I said I'm not.

BOTH.
YOU CAN'T FIRE ME
I QUIT!

VOICE OF CEO. What?!

MARCUS AND DIANE. You can't fire me

JACK AND BRIE. You can't fire me

ALL.
YOU CAN'T FIRE ME! I QUIT!

FELIX. I quit too!

STUART. Freestyle!

ALL. *(A capella, with claps)*
>   YOU CAN'T FIRE ME!
>   YOU CAN'T FIRE ME!
>   YOU CAN'T FIRE ME!
>   I QUIT!
>   YOU CAN'T FIRE ME!
>   YOU CAN'T FIRE ME!
>   YOU CAN'T FIRE ME!
>   I QUIT!

VOICE OF CEO. This is – why you – !

STUART. Look at all this team morale! Hey Mr. CEO, how d'ya like them apples?!

BRIE. What are you gonna do now, you big bully?

MARCUS. Yeah, you gonna go all SOFT on us? Huh?

DIANE. At your age, it's in your demographic profile.

JACK. Consider yourself marginalized!

ALL. *(rolling eyes)* God, Jack…that's lame…*(etc.)*

VOICE OF CEO. Fine! Quit! But you are all alone. It's not like everyone in the audience is going to join in. That would be absolutely ridiculous!

MARCUS. *(to audience)* Wait!
>   YOU'VE BEEN AT YOUR JOBS A LONG LONG TIME

JACK.
>   TO LOSE THEM NOW WOULD BE A CRIME

BRIE.
>   BUT IN THAT TIME WE'VE ALL LEARNED TO BE
>   FRIENDS

DIANE.
>   SO LET'S JUST SING AND GET OUT OF HERE

STUART.
>   THIS BRAND NEW SONG THAT YOU'VE LEARNED BY
>   EAR

ALL.
>   HELP US KICK HIS ASS BY JOINING IN
>   JOINING IN!
>   JOINING IN!!

(The **CAST** *all turn to the audience to join in. Silence...)*

STUART.

YOU CAN'T FIRE ME...COME ON...

(The audience joins in. Finally.)

CAST & AUDIENCE.

YOU CAN'T FIRE ME
YOU CAN'T FIRE ME
YOU CAN'T FIRE ME
I QUIT!

*(***FELIX*** resumes playing.)*

CAST & AUDIENCE. *(cont.)*

YOU CAN'T FIRE ME
YOU CAN'T FIRE ME
YOU CAN'T FIRE ME
I QUIT!

SCENE ELEVEN –
The Denouement or All Is Not What It Seems

VOICE OF CEO. STOP!! Everybody stop singing!

STUART. Oh go to hell.

(The cast begins to exit. The CEO's voice changes slightly.)

VOICE OF CEO. No, really stop! I need to say something.

(The CAST stop in their tracks.)

STUART. Sir?

VOICE OF CEO. It's not me. I mean, I'm not him...the CEO. I'm not really the CEO...

STUART. Kevin?

VOICE OF CEO. Yeah, it's me.

MARCUS. Kevin, I'm gonna kill you!

(EVERYONE starts yelling at KEVIN.)

VOICE OF CEO. Wait! Just wait...everyone, please. This went a lot farther than I wanted it to –

JACK. Why did you do this?!

BRIE. How could you!

VOICE OF CEO. I – I hate Winnipeg!

STUART. You do? I didn't know that.

VOICE OF CEO. Look, I get shit on by customers every day, my girlfriend dumped me because I'm addicted to World of Warcraft and now Stuart – you transferred me to Winnipeg! I just wanted revenge and I'm sorry. I can't ask you to forgive me.

STUART. No, we won't forgive you...But we will thank you. I'd say we all learned a lot from your little prank, right team? I was so busy stressing about making the show work that I lost sight of what was most important; you guys. I'm sorry to see you leave, Kevin. Good bye, and good luck in Winnipeg.

KEVIN. F...U.

SCENE TWELVE – High On a Happy Vibe

(The LCD screen shuts off.)

STUART. Jack, isn't there something you want to say to Brie?

JACK. Brie, I love you.

BRIE. And I love you!

BOTH. We're in love!

(They kiss.)

STUART. Marcus, isn't there something you'd like to say to Diane?

DIANE. Don't even think about.

MARCUS. I'm thinking about the storage closet.

DIANE. I barely remember it.

MARCUS. Oh, you are a wretched, vile woman.

DIANE. And you are a lamentable waste of space.

(They make out.)

STUART. I'm so glad I was here to watch this. In the end, my coworkers fell in love, my team stayed together and my heart didn't explode. I'm so proud of us!

SCENE THIRTEEN – Let's Get Back To Business

SONG – "LET'S GET BACK TO BUSINESS"

STUART.

WE ROSE TO EVERY CHALLENGE
THAT WAS THROWN OUR WAY
WE FOUND OUR OWN TRUE PATH TO WALK
THOUGH WE WERE LED ASTRAY

WE OVERCAME EXTENSIVE ODDS
TO PUT ON QUITE A SHOW
AND NOW TO CELEBRATE OUR FATE
YOU KNOW WHERE WE SHOULD GO?

(Each of the four Chime members shouts out a local hot spot.)

LET'S GET BACK TO BUSINESS
LET'S STOP WASTING TIME
COMPETITORS WILL WET THEIR PANTS
WHEN THEY HEAR OUR CHIME
AND TO EVERYONE WHO LAUGHED AT US, WIPE OFF
THAT GODDAM SMIRK

LET'S GET BACK TO BUSINESS
AND LET'S GET BACK TO WORK

DIANE.

NOW COMING TO WORK, WON'T BE SO DAMN
DEPRESSING

MARCUS.

MORNINGS WE CAN CARPOOL

BOTH.

AND AT LUNCH WE'LL START UNDRESSING

BRIE.

NO MORE SOLO COFFEE BREAKS

JACK.

NO MORE PANICKED HEART ATTACKS

ALL *(ex.* **STUART***)*

WE GOT A WINNING TEAM
SO SCREW WORK, LET'S JUST RELAX!

STUART.

YOUR DAY'S BEEN LONG AND HARD, I ADMIT IT
BUT WE WORK TILL IT'S DONE

ALL.

NO NO NO NO!

STUART.

SO LET'S JUST GET OUT THERE AND DO IT…
AFTER THAT ENTIRE MESS, I'M STILL A LITTLE
STRESSED AND…
DO YOU WANT ME TO FIRE SOMEONE?!

ALL.

LET'S GET BACK GET BACK TO BUSINESS…

LET'S GET BACK GET BACK TO BUSINESS…

LET'S GET BACK GET BACK TO BUSINESS…

LET'S GET BACK GET BACK TO BUSINESS…

STUART.

SO LET'S GET BACK TO BUSINESS!
LET'S GET ON THE RUN!
THERE'S ALWAYS LOTS MORE WORK TO DO
AND OOH AIN'T IT FUN
PEOPLE ARE MORE FUN THAN CASH SO GO ENJOY
THE PERK

ALL.

LET'S GET BACK TO BUSINESS
AND LET'S BACK TO WORK!
THERE'S NOTHING WE CAN'T HANDLE
IF WE FOLLOW THROUGH
(WE FOLLOW THROUGH, OOH)

STUART.

NO OTHER TEAM HOLDS A CANDLE
SO STOP FOOLIN' AROUND, COMMIT TO GETTIN'
DOWN
(LET'S GET BACK, LET'S GET BACK, LET'S GET BACK)
AND SHOW EM WHAT WE CAN DO!

STUART.

12, 1234!

ALL.

> LET'S GET BACK TO BUSINESS
> LET'S WORK UP A SWEAT
> THERE'S TIME TO CHILL, AND WE SURE WILL
> BUT IT AIN'T THAT TIME YET,
> WE HAVE RESPONSIBILITIES, AND WE'RE NOT ONES
> TO SHIRK
> LET'S GET BACK TO BUSINESS, AND LET'S GET BACK
> TO WORK
> LET'S GET BACK TO BUSINESS
> WE REALLY ARE A TEAM, GO TEAM!

STUART.

> I NEED YOU ALL JUST LIKE MY FEET
> REALLY NEED THAT CREAM!

ALL.

> EVERY SECRETARY, CFO, MBA, AND CLERK
> GET RIGHT BACK TO BUSINESS
> AND GET RIGHT BACK…

STUART.

> TO WORK!!!

ALL.

> LET'S GET BACK, GET BACK TO BUSINESS
> GET RIGHT BACK TO WORK!

PROPS LIST

Stack of recipe cards
Cellphone
Acoustic guitar
Coconut bra
Fruit hat
Tango dress
Puppet built out of stapler
Puppet built out of old printer
Three or four grapes
Several bottles of white out
Handfull of pencils
Stickynotes
Several Sharpies
Bottle of white glue
Scissors
Three hold punch
Roll of toilet paper
Wall clock
Printer box
Small notebook

TECHNICAL NOTES

FUNNY BUSINESS utilized extensive use of two LCD monitors mounted on either side of the proscenium. In the original production's small theatre the 42" monitors were more than large enough to be clearly visible by the whole audience. Depending on the size of your theatre you may need to work out some kind of projection alternative.

SET

Our controlling computer was backstage left. It had a video card capable of dual screen output (through one VGA port and one DVI). We were running Windows XP, and the show was a series of cleverly constructed Microsoft Powerpoint slides, with all the necessary media embedded in individual slides. The front of house monitors were connected to a signal splitter which was in turn connected to the DVI port. They were set as the secondary monitor, the backstage one being set as the primary. Within Powerpoint there is the option to display the presentation on external monitors. This allows the slides to be shown to the audience, but leaving the backstage monitor with a "Presenter's view" which contains information about the slides and shows them in order. Once it's set up and working, all that is needed to run the show is the repeated pressing of the right arrow key to move from slide to slide.

OTHER MUSICALS AVAILABLE FROM SAMUEL FRENCH

WILD DUST: THE MUSICAL

Music by Dennis Poore
Book by Flip Kobler & Cindy Marcus
Lyrics by Flip Kobler

Musical Comedy / 1m, 8f, plus 1m extra / Interior

The worst dust storm in a decade is about to hit the town, and all the men have gone to drive the horses and cattle to safer shelter to ride out the dust, leaving the women of town to fend for themselves in the only building strong enough to withstand the pounding sand - the town brothel. So four "ladies of the night" and three "ladies of the…ah….day" are thrown together along with a mysterious cowboy who rides out of the wind. For the next 72 hours our heroes confront the elements, each other, and hardest of all - themselves. It's a comic romp that gives a healthy wink to the days of Gene Autry and Roy Rogers. There's lots of slamming doors, mistaken identities, and one very dead body. No one is exactly what they seem, and everyone's got a secret hidden up their sleeve.

OTHER MUSICALS AVAILABLE FROM SAMUEL FRENCH

DOG PARK: THE MUSICAL

Jahnna Beecham, Malcolm Hillgartner and Michael J. Hume
Music by Malcolm Hillgartner

Comedy / 3m, 1f / Simple Set

Follow Daisy the sassy Westie through her dating adventures with Itchy, Champ and Bogie at the hippest, hottest place in town: Central Bark, where every dog has his day, and love conquers all. Daisy has promised her BFF (Best Friend Forever) she'd give the dating scene one more chance. She meets Champ the Collie, a charming but full of himself show dog; Itchy, a "humperactive" Jack Russell terrier; and Bogie, the darkly mysterious Lab/mutt who sticks his neck out for no one. This unusual quartet make their way through the day's scheduled events which include Singles With Friends, Agility Class, Speed Mating, Yappy Hour and Lovers with Leashes, which is when they pair up and leave the park. Daisy comes to the conclusion that Champ only has eyes for himself, Itchy can only be a friend, and Bogie is the dog for her. But when Daisy makes her desires known to Bogie, she gets a rude awakening; we learn that Bogie, a stray, has been living at the Dogpark for six months. Bogie confesses his love for Daisy just as Animal Control arrives to take him away. Will Bogie and Daisy ever be reunited? Fresh off its sold-out run at Milwaukee Rep comes *Dog Park: The Musical*, created by the team behind the hit *Chaps!* and *Chaps! A Jingle Jangle Christmas!*